W9-AHQ-980

SHIFTY'S
BOYS

Also by Chris Offutt

SHIFTY'S BOYS

A MICK HARDIN NOVEL

CHRIS OFFUTT

Grove Press

New York

Copyright © 2022 by Chris Offutt

All rights reserved. No part of this book may be reproduced in any
form or by any electronic or mechanical means, including information
storage and retrieval systems, without permission in writing from the
publisher, except by a reviewer, who may quote brief passages in a review.
Scanning, uploading, and electronic distribution of this book or the
facilitation of such without the permission of the publisher is prohibited.
Please purchase only authorized electronic editions, and do not
participate in or encourage electronic piracy of copyrighted materials.
Your support of the author's rights is appreciated. Any member
of educational institutions wishing to photocopy part or all of the work
for classroom use, or anthology, should send inquiries to
Grove Atlantic, 154 West 14th Street, New York, NY 10011
or permissions@groveatlantic.com.

FIRST EDITION

Published simultaneously in Canada
Printed in the United States of America

First Grove Atlantic hardcover edition: June 2022

Library of Congress Cataloging-in-Publication data is available for this title.

ISBN 978-0-8021-5998-4
eISBN 978-0-8021-5999-1

Grove Press
an imprint of Grove Atlantic
154 West 14th Street
New York, NY 10011

Distributed by Publishers Group West

groveatlantic.com

22 23 24 25   10 9 8 7 6 5 4 3 2 1

For Sam Offutt

These hills don't change.

—Cesare Pavese

Chapter One

At age eight, Albin decided to be a race-car driver when he grew up. He assembled model cars, cobbling together pieces from various kits to make his own hot rod—number eleven, painted in green and white. He imagined himself as the youngest winner of the Brickyard 400, with enough money for ice cream every meal. It never occurred to him that at twenty-two years old he'd be driving a cab in his hometown of Rocksalt, Kentucky.

Half the job was sitting in the car waiting for dispatch to call. The rest was driving roads he'd traveled thousands of times in the past eight years—blacktop, dirt, and gravel. A county map was imprinted on the inside of his skull. All he had to do was mentally glance at it to know the best route. He had a few regular fares, severely inebriated men leaving the only two bars in town. The bulk of his customers needed a ride to a doctor's office or home from the hospital. He relied on them for income and felt momentarily disappointed when they recovered, which he knew said something awful about himself.

For the past six hours he'd been on duty with no calls. He cruised the small college campus, worthless at night, but he was bored and getting desperate. Main Street was deserted. He drove by the new jail, another waste of time because nobody got released after dark. The bars were just getting active, and it'd be several hours before the drunks started leaving. He called dispatch to double-check that his cell phone was working and got chewed out for tying up the line.

Rocksalt had a few places that were suitable to waiting for a fare. A drugstore parking lot in the middle of town was best, but twice he'd been stiffed by pillbillies who'd spent all their money on legally prescribed opiates. It was time to find an isolated spot, take two hits off a joint, and enter his long-term fantasy of being a race-car driver. All it took was a big-shot promoter passing through to hire his cab and recognize Albin's skill at the wheel.

He'd bought his first go-cart at Western Auto, a company that went out of business several years ago. Albin had loved entering the store from the rear and descending the steps to the sales floor. It was the only indoor vista in the county, one he'd marveled at as a teenager. Now the asphalt parking lot behind the store was pocked with holes, some deep enough to damage his car's suspension. Fast-food bags littered the surface along with empty pop bottles. He carefully steered to his favorite place, snugged against the old door, its glass replaced by a sheet of plywood. The roof cast a shadow that would conceal his cab. An odd shape lay in a corner of the lot, and Albin flicked on his brights. Somebody was sleeping against the dilapidated fence, somebody who could use a ride home.

Albin left the car, something no cabbie liked to do, and walked toward the man, who lay on his back. One arm was twisted beneath him, the other outstretched as if reaching toward Albin. Dark splotches marred his clothing. Albin thought it was mud until getting closer and recognizing dried blood. He stumbled to his car and called 911. Then he hid the half joint in the cell phone charging slot built into the dashboard, glad he hadn't smoked before the cops arrived.

Chapter Two

Mick Hardin awoke from a dream in which he lay in his childhood bed and couldn't move. His eyelids felt weighted, and he wondered if he was already dead and someone had placed pennies over his eyes. The coins were supposed to hold eyelids shut and serve as payment to the ferryman who transported the dead across the River Styx. Mick lay awake remembering the IED attack that had sent him to an army hospital for three weeks. He'd been released and ordered to rehabilitate his leg, a grueling and painful ordeal. From bed he'd moved to a wheelchair, then shifted to crutches for three months. He'd graduated to a cane that embarrassed him in public.

His commanding officer, Colonel Whitaker, presented him with a special cane intended for soldiers. The lightweight aluminum was painted black, with a slogan down one side: "This We'll Defend." Because the words were printed vertically, the apostrophe was a tiny pip, and the

motto appeared at first glance to be "This Well Defend."
Every time Mick used it, he remembered the old well at his
grandfather's cabin in the woods, the water cold enough to
numb his gums. He rehabbed his leg until he could limp
around the base on his own, then asked to go home for the
rest of his medically mandated leave. His wife would look
after him and could drive him to the nearest VA hospital,
eighty miles away in Lexington. The colonel agreed and
ordered Mick to keep his cell phone on and return all calls.
Mick nodded and flew home.

Now he opened his eyes. He was in his mother's house,
not the cabin where he'd spent his formative years. He felt
fatigued, his limbs heavy, a product of the pain medication.
He'd gone from fentanyl on the battlefield to morphine in
the hospital to Percocet upon discharge. He was still taking it, although the pain no longer required that level of
management.

He'd lied to Colonel Whitaker. There was no wife
to provide Mick's care. They'd separated a year ago. The
divorce papers were in Mick's luggage, unsigned, along
with his cell phone, switched off. He was waiting for a
reason to complete the documents and sever himself from
sixteen years of marriage. Despite the circumstances, it
didn't feel right. Neither did sleeping at his mother's house
in a spare room. Mick's sister, Linda, had inherited the
house when their mother died. Linda was at work. She
was county sheriff, running for election, and he didn't see
her much.

The bedside clock said ten thirty, and Mick knew she'd be home for lunch soon. He had enough time to walk his daily two miles for the reward of Percocet. He left the ranch house at the deadend of Lyons Avenue and set a strong pace. In several neighboring yards were clumps of forsythia that glowed yellow, cheerful in the spring sun, their fronds already tinged green along the edges. Jonquils were blooming. On the hill overlooking the street, he could see the haze of redbud and a few pink dogwoods. The hills were gorgeous in all seasons, especially spring, when the land offered such promise and hope. Its beauty plowed him under. Mick's life had come undone to a great degree, and here he was licking his wounds under his dead mother's roof, tended to by his tough sister. The absurdity of the situation cheered him momentarily.

A neighbor woman waved from her flower bed. Two dogs trotted around another house, the entire back half of their bodies wiggling a greeting. He gave them a walking scratch, reluctant to break his stride. His leg hurt, but it felt good to put his limbs to work. He was mostly healed. Daily exercise was the final stage of rehab, intended to rebuild the muscle mass he'd lost from lying for weeks in grim hospital beds. Across the street was Miller, the mail carrier, a man Mick knew from high school. His was one of the few federal jobs in the county, and more than four hundred people had applied. Everybody wondered how Miller had gotten the position.

Mick silently cursed his bad timing—now he'd have to chat with every person on the street who was retrieving their mail. Sure enough, Old Man Boyle lingered by his box, watching Mick approach. He wore creased trousers, tan loafers, and a shirt buttoned to the collar, as if he'd dressed for the occasion of leaving the house. Bull Boyle had served in Vietnam and lost a son in Iraq. He maintained a certain sympathy for Mick, wrapped in a shroud of resentment that Mick had come home more or less intact. Above each of Boyle's ears was a large crescent-shaped hearing aid of a vague tan color. Mick recognized them as old-school VA issue.

"How's the wheel?" Boyle said, pointing to Mick's leg.

Mick slowed to an amble out of respect.

"Getting stronger every day," he said. "Any good mail?"

"Yeah, I won two thousand dollars. Got to go to the Chevy dealer to collect. They'll give me a sales pitch, then a pair of earbuds. What the hell am I going to do with them? Side of my head'll look like a hardware store with all manner of equipment hanging off it."

Mick chuckled.

"Your sister all right?" Boyle said.

"Yeah, she's running me ragged. Only reason I do my walks is to get her off my ass."

"She's a good lawman-woman," Boyle said. "I'll vote for her."

"Linda said it'll be close."

"That other feller's no good. Thinks he's shit on a stick and would be if he had a peg leg." He glanced again at Mick's leg. "Didn't mean nothing by that."

"I know it, Mr. Boyle. I got to get on before it stiffens up on me."

"Good man," he said. "Catch you on the flip-flop."

Mick increased his pace, listening for the faintly audible pop of his knee or the imaginary creak in his hip. As the crow flies, it was a quarter mile from his sister's house to the first cross street, but Lyons Avenue followed a meandering creek off the hills and the route was ultimately a full mile. Twice he crossed the street to avoid people.

Their father died young, and Linda had stayed with their mother. From age eight, Mick had lived with his grandfather and great-grandfather in the woods twelve miles east. He'd never liked town. It wasn't Rocksalt specifically but clusters of people in general. Town required a social patina he was no good at, an exoskeleton of politesse. People said one thing and meant another. They became offended if you dared to be honest and direct. It was as if saying what you thought was forbidden. He preferred the forthrightness of country people and army life.

Lyons Avenue ended at Second Street, a name that always amused Mick due to its lack of imagination. In big cities, such designations made sense because of multiple cross streets, but Rocksalt had only three: Main Street, First Street, and Second Street. Mick made his turn and walked back toward his sister's house. Two cars passed, and he waved without looking. Sweat skimmed his back and legs. He was breathing easily enough to escalate his pace to a forced march, eyes straight ahead and alert to the periphery. His sister's house came into view, and he double-timed it, counting cadence in his head, one hundred and eighty steps per minute, until he made it to the driveway.

Panting like a dog, he leaned against the exterior wall and drank from the garden hose, pleased with his progress. He was nearly strong enough to return to duty. His wife of sixteen years was living in another town with another man and their child. At best he considered it collateral damage from prolonged deployments overseas. At worst, he'd failed as a husband.

Chapter Three

Sheriff Linda Hardin drove the county vehicle home for lunch with her brother. She loved Lyons Avenue, where she'd grown up. She'd learned to ride a bicycle here, gone door-to-door selling Christmas candles to raise money for her grade school, and later sneaked out for furtive cigarettes with a neighbor girl. Linda knew all the neighbors, none of whom would have predicted that she'd be the first female sheriff in county history. A natural lead foot, she always drove slowly on her own street so everyone could see the big SUV with the official decal emblazoned on the doors and a light bar across the top.

She'd had a busy morning that amounted to nothing—an empty car parked on a dirt road off Big Brushy, unintelligible graffiti on a barn, and four wild dogs chasing a loose cow. She had a court appearance in the afternoon. Not a bad life for a single woman with a good paycheck. The only drawback was her brother, who seemed to be recovered from the IED attack in Afghanistan but was still taking pills and rarely leaving the house. His presence was a palpable force, as if he filled the entire space with his wounded psyche. She loved him but preferred living alone.

She drove into her driveway and saw him leaning against the clapboards, spraying the back of his head with the hose. Water formed a cone around his face like a veil. It was as close to a bath as he'd had for days.

"Hey, Mick," she said. "Glad to see you're cleaning up some."

He nodded, making the fan of water shiver like a shower curtain. She went into the house for a towel, noting with a grimace that they were all clean and folded, as they had been for a week. She took it outside.

"I don't want you dripping in the house," she said.

He turned off the hose and nodded his thanks.

"Been meaning to ask," she said, "how come you quit taking showers? Your leg?"

"No," he said.

"Well, it's getting on my last nerve."

"Wish you'd told me that three or four nerves ago."

She chuckled.

"Well," she said, "why not?"

"I took a shower every day in the army, sometimes twice. Part of it was dust in the desert. But the real reason was never knowing when I'd have access to plumbing again."

"Yeah, so?"

"You've always got running water. Knowing I can take a shower anytime means I don't have to."

"That doesn't make a lot of sense, Big Bro."

"No, I guess not," he said. "Not much does anymore."

"That's your pills talking. Why're you still on them anyway?"

"Because I'm stuck here living with you instead of my wife. And it's better than drinking whiskey."

"Maybe it's time to go back."

"To whiskey?"

"No, to Germany and the base. The life you like."

"Not yet," he said.

He walked away, rubbing the towel briskly over his head. Linda watched him go. She worried about him, but he was a big boy, and she was more concerned with her career. Several years ago, Linda had become a dispatcher for the sheriff's office. To her surprise, she liked being part of something bigger than herself, something that was good for the county. When a deputy resigned under a sexual harassment scandal, she was offered the position. The county politicians thought the first female deputy would help offset the negative publicity. Linda reluctantly agreed, mainly for the bump in pay. The sheriff died suddenly, and she was promoted past the senior deputy, a lazy and incompetent nitwit who worked part-time at a landfill, where he'd managed to wreck three dump trucks, no easy task. He quit the force, and Linda appointed Johnny Boy Tolliver as deputy and learned the job.

She'd never intended to run for sheriff. Her plan had been to fill the post until the election, then ask the winner for reassignment back to dispatch, but a sexist moron had thrown his hat in the ring. Keeping him out of the job was crucial to her. If he won the election, it would vindicate all the men who thought a woman shouldn't have authority.

Most important, she was good at the job. Everyone knew her family history—father a drunk, mother a shut-in, brother with personal problems and hard to get along with. In Eldridge County this public information made her trustworthy. She believed she could win the election as long as her brother didn't cause social friction. On the surface he was calm and calculating, but she knew he was capable of sudden action based on intuition. Nobody could control him. Maybe she should confiscate opiates from a dealer and make sure Mick had plenty. Drugged, he wouldn't be at risk of interfering in the election. Ideally she'd arrest him for possession and ship him back to base. Grinning to herself, she went inside.

Mick had made lunch—turkey and Swiss sandwiches with potato chips and pop. A slight tension tinged their silence. He ate as if in a mess hall, arms protecting his plate, eyes on the food. Linda searched her mind for a subject to ease things, difficult because so many crucial topics were forbidden—his wife, his wounds, the drugs, now even his damn hygiene.

"Oh," she said. "Some local news I need to tell you."

He nodded, chewing.

"A body was found two days ago."

"Just the one?"

"That's right, smart guy. Thing is, you know him."

She waited for him to display curiosity about the world beyond his concerns. Instead he looked at her, waiting.

"It was Fuckin' Barney," she said.

"He still moving heroin in?"

"Well," she said, "not as of two days ago."

His quick grin was like a sudden burst of sunlight emerging from behind a rain cloud then vanishing. She felt triumphant.

"Who do you like for it?" he said.

"Nobody. It's city cop jurisdiction. He was behind Western Auto. Shot three times."

"Thought it was closed."

"It is," she said. "This ain't about the store."

"What's it about, then?"

"Dope," she said. "What else? Now wash them dishes for me, will you? And take a damn shower. I've got court."

She stood up from the Formica table, adjusted her equipment belt, and left. Mick wondered what she was riled up about. A good soldier, he followed her orders, then took a Percocet and lay on the couch. He had one more pill left. He could save it or take it now. He took it. He'd regret it tomorrow when he wanted one, but the regrets were piled up like cordwood everywhere he looked. His medical leave ended soon. Better if he was off the meds then anyhow. Still, the days would pass even more slowly without pills.

The opiates hit him—not nearly as hard as he'd like but enough to flatten his sense of time. The light through the window was pretty to look at.

Chapter Four

Four days later Mick felt ninety percent healed. The daily fog of fatigue had faded with the absence of Percocet. He'd squelched the wanton cravings, not so much for opiates or whiskey but for escape itself. Mick supposed he was lucky—he liked to drink, and now he knew he enjoyed narcotics, but he lacked the addiction gene. He could turn it off like throwing a switch. The first couple of days were tough. Much tougher was the knowledge that the switch was always within reach, ready to be flicked back on.

Inactivity was his nemesis, and he walked twice a day for a longer distance, getting in three miles, then five and six. His leg hurt only at night. He tidied the house and showered daily, which improved relations with his sister. Everyone else in their family was dead. Neither of them had kids. It was just them, and he may as well get along with her. He decided to try television, but it was all sex and zombies, serial killers and sad cops. The comedies weren't funny. He found a documentary on Atlantis, a place that might have existed but nobody knew where. It consisted of a great many shots of the ocean, and he wondered how it qualified as a documentary.

Someone knocked at the front door, an anomaly since most people used the side entrance off the kitchen. Mick paused the TV show and opened the door to Mason Kissick. They appraised each other in the way of country men in town, neither quite comfortable with the circumstances, both waiting for the other to react. Mason lowered his chin in greeting.

"Mick," he said.

"Mason."

With the initial phase over, another minute passed while Mick tried to figure out why Fuckin' Barney's brother was here. Mason stood as if he were a tree with not a care in the world.

"Heard you got shot over there," Mason said.

"Naw, I got blowed up. An IED."

"Damn. I had a girlfriend with one of them in her. Didn't know they could blow up. Hurt your peter any?"

"It's a kind of bomb, Mason. What do you want?"

"Ain't me, it's Mommy. She wants to talk to you."

"Well, bring her in, then."

"She won't come to town. Sent me to fetch you out to the house."

"The last time me and her talked, it wasn't on good terms."

"She said to tell you that's done with now."

"What's on her mind, Mason?"

"Nope." He shook his head. "She said she'll tell you her own self."

Mick considered the expedition. The only times he'd gone anywhere was the drugstore or the hospital. He'd made one trip for clothes to his old house, empty after his wife moved out. He became so morose he swore never to return. Driving to the far side of the county might do him some good.

Mason operated his Taurus with great care, clearly new to the complexities of driving in town. His way of dealing with stop signs was to sneak up on them gradually with a few tentative halts, then a long wait at the sign itself. Fully satisfied that he was safe, he entered the intersection with sudden acceleration, then a quick application of the brakes as if to avoid any last-minute vehicle that had escaped his vigilance. Mick stared out the window. He'd driven with worse drivers in the army. The absolute worst were civilian contractors in Iraq.

The pale green of spring lay over the land, each recent bud straining toward the sun. There was a palpable energy in the hills from the trees still in flower, the opening leaves of softwoods, and the infant animals—fawns and kits and naive young snakes. The light had a gentle quality, the sky pastel. Mick felt good to be out of the house and in motion, to have a destination, even if it was Mason's mother. The last time he'd seen Mrs. Kissick, they'd both been armed. She was a hard woman.

Mason left the blacktop for the dirt lane that led to his mother's house.

"Hey," Mick said. "Should've told you before. I'm sorry about your brother."

"Thanks," Mason said. "Just so you know, Mommy don't want us calling him Fuckin' Barney no more. He's Barney now. Just Barney."

Mick nodded. Death was a force of social leveling in the hills, a provider of intricate respect. He recalled a woman who'd married a man her parents despised in life. When he died young, they'd buried him in their family cemetery.

Mason drove into the yard and parked near the three board steps to a porch that spanned the front of the house. The holler received less light than town, and the yard oak held a few blossoms. Grass was scanty. They climbed the steps and entered the house.

Shifty Kissick sat in a reclining chair with a lever repaired by duct tape, antimacassars draped over each arm. On a low table beside her were an ashtray, a cup of coffee, and a small pistol that lacked a front sight to avoid snagging on clothes. Mick had seen her friendly and threatening but never the way she was now—dour with pain, her eyes blazing like a blast furnace. He waited for her to speak. Instead she gestured to a chair.

"Mason," she said, "get the man some coffee."

"I'm sorry for your loss, Mrs. Kissick," Mick said.

She nodded, so accustomed to hearing the platitude that it slid past her like grease. She'd lost two of her five kids, both boys, one to a car wreck many years back, and now Barney murdered. Mason brought a cup of coffee, black and steaming, in a mug emblazoned with a cheerful cow. Out of respect, Mick held it in a way to conceal the bovine smile. The front room was tidy, containing a couch, two chairs, a wide-screen TV with a gaming setup, and a paint-by-numbers depiction of The Last Supper in a filigree frame. Another wall held a faded color photograph of Shifty and her late husband. They looked happy. Mick sipped the harsh coffee and nodded, waiting.

"You still in the service?" Shifty said.

"Yes, ma'am. On leave till my leg's good."

"How much longer?"

"Depends on the doc. But not too long, a week or so."

She nodded, and he understood that she knew all this already. She probably knew about his wife and the baby, too. He wondered if she knew about the Percocet. He sat quietly, waiting. Hill culture didn't traffic in the surface tedium of chatting nicely with people. She'd sent for him. He was here. It was on her now, and he'd wait until she got to the reason behind the summons.

"I need some help," she said.

He nodded, surprised. She was down a boy, but Mick wasn't about to step into the drug-dealing gap left by the

death of Fuckin' Barney. He glanced at Mason, her youngest son, a man who required precise instructions. Perhaps
she needed some work done on the land. It would be good
exercise, and Mason could drive him around.

"What kind of help, Mrs. Kissick?"

"Find out who killed Barney."

"You need to talk to the city police."

"I done did," she said. "Till I was blue in the face.
They've got their mind made up."

The pupils of her eyes had constricted with anger. Her
right eye focused on his right eye, a sign of aggression. Mick
nodded and studied the coffee cup.

"What did the police tell you?" he said.

"To stop aggravating them."

"What about going through a lawyer? They'll know
the right way to talk to the cops."

"I can't," she said.

"Can't or won't?"

"Both but mostly can't."

"Sounds kind of tricky."

"It is," she said. "Barney always was, even dead. I'll
pay you good money."

He leaned back and opened his posture, focusing his
left eye on her right to ease her off a little. His voice was
modulated low and slow.

"Mrs. Kissick," he said, "I can't agree to anything until
I know more."

"Like what?"

"What the cops said. Why you don't believe them. Who you think killed your son."

Her silence manufactured a rigidity that hung in the air. She looked about the room like a wild animal trapped in a corner. Shifty was in her late fifties with long dark hair. Two streaks of gray ran along her temples and converged in the back. She leaned forward, and Mick prepared for a sudden attack. Instead she sprang to her feet, agile as a child.

"Outside," she said. "Mason, you stay in here."

Mick followed her to the porch. They sat on wooden chairs facing the road and Mason's red Taurus. She lit a cigarette and cuffed her jeans for an ashtray.

"Smoke?" she said.

"Naw, I quit. I do miss them, though."

"They're no good," she said, "but a comfort at times. About like Barney."

"What did the cops say?"

"Drug deal gone bad."

"Maybe it was."

"Nope, not in town. He was smart that way. Did all his business out in the county."

"Girlfriend. Girlfriend's husband. Somebody's ex?"

"He didn't have nobody regular. Didn't want anything complicated. He had a few lady friends he'd visit. Regular ones. He wasn't a hound dog like some."

A slow blush rose from her neck and suffused her face. The subject of physical intimacy was uncomfortable.

"He talked to you about that?" Mick said.

"Once. He was drunk and smoking on the weed. He apologized for not giving me no grandbabies. I told him it didn't matter, his sister's got four kids. But he felt bad about it. My oldest boy's got a Mexican woman in California. No kids. Mason, he had one girlfriend five or six years ago, didn't last a month. Barney thought it was on him to carry the Kissick name. He wanted me to know why he was single."

"What was it he said?"

"My husband died young, and it was hard on the family. Barney didn't want to do his wife and kids that way. He was going to make his money and get out. He liked wrestling, that WWE stuff. He talked about organizing some fights. He could have done that. Had the mind for it."

Her voice trailed off. She stubbed the cigarette against the gray slats of the porch and lit another. A robin with a piece of bright moss clenched in its beak flew to an old woodpile in the yard. It landed on the thick bark of a hickory, jerked its head as if checking for surveillance, then stepped into a space between two logs.

"They build a new nest every year," Mick said.

"I know it. I seen them feed other birds' young. They're a generous bird."

"What I like, they sing all year long."

They watched the woodpile for a couple of minutes. A cloud passed in front of the sun, dimming the light like gauze. Mick felt comfortable sitting with her. She blew smoke that caught a breeze.

"Well," she said. "Will you do it?"

"I know it's hard, Mrs. Kissick, and you're upset about it. What I don't understand is why you don't just leave it to the police."

"Far as they're concerned, Barney was a drug dealer who got what's coming to him."

"You sure about that?"

"Yep. A boy in the Rocksalt Police Department used to date my daughter ten years back. He told me the case is open, but they ain't looking for nobody."

"What's the cop's name?"

"Nope." She shook her head. "I ain't a snitch."

"Was Barney?"

She jerked her head to him, her gaze a flat wind leveling everything in its path. Sunlight reflected from her eyes like sparks off flint. Her voice was harsh.

"Snitches get stitches and wind up in ditches shitting their britches."

Mick nodded. He sat quietly to let her anger pass. She put the cigarette out and lit another.

"If you want my help," Mick said, "I have to ask questions like that."

She gathered a long breath, exhaled, then sucked on the cigarette.

"That mean you'll do it?"

"Why me?"

"I don't trust the law."

"I'm an army cop, ma'am. Special agent in the CID."

"I don't see no army around here."

"You're not answering the question," he said. "Why me?"

"I half trust you," she said in a quiet voice.

"Why?"

"Because you don't care."

Mick thought about that. She was right—he didn't care about her son or the law. Murder in the hills led to more killing, and he only cared that people had the chance to live, not die.

"Tell you what," he said. "I'll dig around a little. If I think there's something off, I'll look more. But if I don't, I'm done. And I don't want you getting mad about it. You understand what I mean?"

"Yes, I understand. I'm a damn grieving mother, not some kind of stupid idiot."

"Who do you think did it?"

"I don't know," she said, voice suddenly forlorn. "That's all I set here thinking about. But I can't think who."

Mick stood and nodded to her.

"Thank you for the coffee. Will you get Mason to run me home?"

She called her son's name and gestured to his car. Mason slowly negotiated the dirt lane and reached the main road to town. The lush spring buds of softwood trees rose beyond the ditch, the oaks and hickories still in blossom.

"Who do you think killed Barney?" Mick said.

"What'd Mommy say?"

"She didn't know."

"I don't either."

Mick nodded, recognizing the stubborn loyalty of the hills. An hour later they'd completed the sixteen-mile journey to Rocksalt, during which Mason said nothing more. He was a good son. He'd never betray his family or get a ticket for speeding.

Chapter Five

Johnny Boy Tolliver sat in his deputy's office admiring the contours of the room. Battered filing cabinets lined the walls. They contained case files that ran back seven decades, neatly filed by year, then alphabetized by last name of victim. He'd organized them into three groups—active cases, repeat offenders, and unsolved murders. The last file was very slim, but he read it once a month due to a personal interest. His cousin was in there, Billy Rodale, murdered twenty-five years back, and nobody arrested. Johnny Boy regarded the files as a history of the county. He was an archival librarian who got to carry a sidearm.

As deputy, he was spared the necessity of hanging a fake oil portrait of the governor on the wall. Instead he'd hung a reproduction of the earliest map of "Kentucke," from 1784, the eastern edge of which included present-day Eldridge County. One shelf held a slew of books about the state. One gave details to every formally designated emblem, motto, and symbol. He'd been astounded by a few choices, such as milk being the official state beverage. It should have been Ale-8, Kentucky's only native soft drink.

His computer was bulky and slow, fifteen years old. A short wire ran to a printer that confounded him on a regular basis. It was like a recalcitrant mule that refused to budge for reasons of its own—fatigue, boredom, or perhaps a child-like rebellion. Beside it a push-button phone connected the line to the sheriff and the new dispatcher. A single personal item sat on the edge of his desk, a framed photograph he'd taken with his cell phone two years ago. It depicted Linda arresting her brother. It had been in the county newspaper and the *Lexington Herald-Leader*. He was proud of the photo, though secretly disappointed that it hadn't gone viral.

Linda was in court, and the new dispatcher was at lunch, which left Johnny Boy in charge, a situation he enjoyed. One call had come in earlier, an older woman with dementia spotted in a fallow field. He knew Mrs. Hayes, her adult kids and grandchildren, even a few great-grands. Periodically she walked to the house where she'd first lived with her husband sixty years before. Johnny Boy picked her up and drove her home. A teenage girl answered the door and said, "Granny gets out sometimes. She's like a cat."

Now Johnny Boy sat in his office considering lunch. Options were few in a town of six thousand. Chinese, Mexican, pizza, or hamburgers. Everybody raved about the new Cracker Barrel on the interstate, but he thought it was too cluttered with junk nailed to the walls. Worse, the last woman he'd dated worked there. It had been seven years, but he still felt a jolt of loss when he saw her. No sense getting sad at lunch.

He'd settled on a meal at Coffee Tree, a bookstore that sold sandwiches and yarn. Out of habit he checked his trash can, vacant because he'd emptied it twice already. Some days were so slow he wadded up paper and threw it away so he'd need to dump the garbage.

Sheriff Hardin entered the front door, moving fast as usual, her boots battering the worn carpet. She went into her office, and he stood in the door.

"How was court?" he said.

"Three months jail, credit for time served. He's out."

"The meth guy? Don't seem right."

"Three things in his favor. His meth lab was a van parked in the woods. It blew up, and they couldn't prove it was his. Second, he had nothing on him at his arrest."

"What's the third thing?"

"He's a Ryan on his mom's side. Different laws for different families."

"Them Ryans are so stuck up they'd drown in a hard rain."

She didn't react to his joke, and he understood that her level of irritability was running high. He quickly informed her of the morning's call to retrieve Mrs. Hayes. Linda grunted, looking through paperwork.

"I got something for you to do," she said.

"I was just heading out for lunch."

"Well, you can eat on the way. You need to run Mick up to Papaw's old cabin. He wants his truck."

"That doesn't sound like official business."

"It's not, but I'll let you take the SUV. He's at my house. You two can eat on the way."

"Is that an order?"

"No, damn it, it's a favor. I've got to go on some campaign runs."

"I don't think Mick likes me much."

"He doesn't like anybody much."

She tossed him the keys. He caught them with the grace of an athlete and jingled them, his face delighted.

"Don't wreck it," she said.

In the parking lot Johnny Boy encountered the dispatcher returning from lunch. Sandra Caldwell was in her mid-thirties, brown-headed, smart, and organized. She'd recently broken up with a boyfriend, and Johnny Boy nourished a fervent hope that she'd take an interest in him. It'd be one of those office romances maintained in secret until they announced their wedding, and everyone would be happy for them.

Sandra nodded to him without slowing as she entered the sheriff's office. He watched her go, thinking that he needed to figure out a way to talk to her beyond relaying operational information.

Johnny Boy cruised town twice, following the route that teenagers took on Friday nights. As usual, the sidewalk was mostly deserted, except for two old men sitting on a bench. One appeared to be asleep, and the other was blind. Johnny Boy waved anyway, a curt gesture befitting his status operating the official vehicle. He drove to Linda's house and honked twice. Mick left the side door and crossed through the carport to the passenger side.

"Heard you were in," Johnny Boy said. "Sorry you got hurt over there."

"Getting better."

"Where to?"

"East on Old Sixty."

"You a'caring if we stop and eat? Maybe a drive-through."

Mick nodded and sat quietly as they drove through town and ordered fast food. Johnny Boy ate one-handed from his lap while heading deeper into the hills. Mick seemed to relax after they left Rocksalt, staring through the window at the cheerful pale green of softwood buds. An occasional cardinal sliced the air like a streak of blood.

"Something I learned the other day," Johnny Boy said. "Been worrying me. The Kentucky state rock is agate. And the state mineral is coal. But here's the thing, coal ain't a mineral, it's a rock. And agate, it's a mineral, not rock. They got that backwards. How'd that happen?"

"Go right at Bearskin Holler."

Slightly stung by being ignored, Johnny Boy made the turn onto a narrow blacktop lane with patches of dirt showing through the tar. The county had paved it once with as little asphalt as possible, a way to save money and

garner votes. Judging by the condition of the road, Johnny
Boy figured it was at least two elections back. He veered
around mud holes that sprouted tall grass. The road began
a gradual ascent into heavier woods. Maple branches inter-
twined with sunshine filtering through in a shifting kalei-
doscope of light. The blacktop petered out to dirt, then a
pair of ruts. Johnny Boy stopped the car.

"You sure this is right?" he said.

"On foot from here. About a half mile."

"Your leg make it?"

Mick left the SUV and began walking. Johnny Boy
climbed out, locked it, then double-checked the lock
and hurried up the hill. A crow called a warning. Two
chickadees halted their talk. He could hear his boots on
the tamped-down dirt but not Mick's, which puzzled him.
Maybe a bad leg made him walk quiet.

At the top of the hill, the ruts became a road again,
overgrown by fescue, milkweed, and the drooping flowers of
ground-cherry. The land opened to a clear area, surrounded
by a wall of trees. Johnny Boy hadn't been up here before, but
he'd heard about it from Linda—the hundred-year-old cabin
where Mick grew up. The original structure was built of log
chinked with clay mud, replaced by gray rows of cement. It
had two additions cobbled on like wings. The flue from a
woodstove rose above the roof, and a single gutter ran to a
rain barrel. Beyond it stood an old smokehouse leaning backward, as if gravity was pulling it down the hill.

A 1960s-era pickup truck was parked in front of the cabin. All four tires were flat. The weight of the engine had pressed the front tires so hard the rubber had split. Twigs and dead grass spilled from a crevice in the tire where small animals had denned up, probably mice. Mick opened the truck and tried the engine. Nothing, not even a steady click. Johnny Boy's mood dropped as he realized he'd be stuck driving Mick around. He hoped somebody out in the county committed a crime—and soon.

Mick circled the cabin as if reconnoitering his home, moving as silently as he had on the walk. Johnny Boy made a mental note to ask about that technique, then followed Mick into the house. The place was a wreck of empty beer cans, cigarette butts, broken glass and crockery. Empty fast-food bags lay in a corner as if blown by wind. A few books were scattered on the floor. It reminded Johnny Boy of the aftermath of parties he'd attended during college, the residue of heedless behavior by young men. Mick peered in each room, then picked up an empty package of rolling papers.

"Somebody been partying in here," Johnny Boy said. "Was it locked?"

"Never was. Papaw didn't believe in locks."

"Want me to help you clean it up?"

Mick nodded, giving him a look of slight surprise at the offer. Johnny Boy was surprised himself, but the situation called for it. They worked for an hour, filling three large plastic garbage bags and an empty cardboard box intended for twelve bottles of bourbon.

"Funny," Johnny Boy said, "I don't see no empty whiskey bottles."

"They're in the woods. Mine from a year ago."

"Didn't know you drank."

"I don't. But when I do, I make up for all the not."

Johnny Boy frowned, working out the meaning. It was hard to imagine Mick drunk. Probably best that he drank alone out here.

"I never liked bars," Johnny Boy said. "Too bright and loud and full of people. Makes me anxious, then I want to drink more. Worse is all the drunks trying to talk to you."

Mick nodded. They went outside and stood in what passed for a yard. It was a pretty spot, peaceful, catching full sun. Songbirds had returned to their work, no longer concerned by the presence of humans.

"No tire tracks," Johnny Boy said. "If they walked in, it was probably high school kids."

"Good observing."

Johnny Boy momentarily preened beneath the casual praise, then remembered it was his job after all.

"You don't seem that upset about the cabin," he said.

"It's been setting empty. Young boys will go in anything that's not locked tight. I don't blame them. Getting mad would be like two fleas fighting over which one owns the dog. Something my papaw used to say."

"My cousin can get your truck running. Somebody being here would keep the kids away."

"I'd have to meet him first."

They walked back to the SUV. Johnny Boy backed it half a mile, enjoying the use of the rear camera until a curve threw him off and he nearly clipped a buckthorn tree. At the first wide spot he made a three-point turn and headed for the blacktop. He drove west on the main road toward his cousin's house.

"You hear about Fuckin' Barney?" Mick said.

"Somebody killed him."

"Think there's anything unusual about it?"

Johnny Boy was flattered to have his opinion sought. If Mick was asking, he probably thought something was off, and Johnny Boy turned it over in his mind, trying to find what Mick was after. Two miles later it hit him like a load of gravel sliding off a shovel.

"He was shot three times," Johnny Boy said. "Right in the middle of town. Nobody heard the gunfire."

"What's that tell you?"

"They used a silencer."

"Or the body got moved," Mick said. "Any chance you could get hold of the police report? I know it's out of your jurisdiction."

"Heck, I already got it. It's at the office."

"They gave it to you?"

"I got a copy from a buddy. I like to keep all my files up-to-date."

Mick nodded. The spring sun imbued the air with soft light. They passed a thicket of pussy willow, the silver buds already open.

"My guess," Mick said, "some politician had a bunch of agate on his land. He figured if he called it the state rock, it'd be worth some money."

"Uh-huh."

"The word 'mine' means a tunnel. You have to dig one to get minerals. When they started mining coal in a tunnel, they called coal a mineral."

"What makes you to know all that?"

"You ain't the only in these hills to read a book."

Johnny Boy smiled, pleased with himself. He was finally making headway with his boss's cranky brother.

Chapter Six

Jacky Turner muttered to himself, a lifelong habit according to his mother, as he worked in a small outbuilding. Broad sagging shelves held stacks of boxes labeled with their contents—cogs and wheels, turtle shells, mummified birds, good metal, short wire, flotsam, jetsam, and tin patches. Below them was a workbench and containers of bolts, each threaded with the appropriate nut. Jacky liked to organize. It helped focus his hands while he mulled over his inventions. He'd always thought creatively, solving simple problems, but so far none of his ideas had caught on. Most recently he'd developed a razor with a short blade. It was intended for men who needed to shave around acne, also valuable for carefully trimming a precisely designed mustache. One prototype included a small mirror so a man could see his sideburns and keep them even.

His ideas were for the good of the world, but the world wasn't interested—yet. A wheelbarrow that would never tip

over. A leaf blower that made no sound. A special attach-
ment for a hand drill that ensured the screw always stayed
straight. His current project had come to him after driving by a fitness center, the first one in Rocksalt. Jacky had
stopped his car, backed up, and peered inside for an hour.
Eight people were riding stationary bicycles nowhere. All
that kinetic energy wasted on health.

Since then he'd been working on a means to harness
the energy, convert it to electricity, and store it in cells. It
would be valuable in the future when the power grid failed
and nothing worked. People could ride stationary bikes to
generate their own electricity.

He left the shed for the house and rummaged through
his storage area—living room, bedroom, and half the
pantry—looking for a low-watt light bulb. His father was
bedridden with emphysema, and his mother watched television. Her favorites were game shows that involved the
humiliation of contestants, a preference Jacky never understood. She mainly tended to her husband's needs, which
gave Jacky the run of the house. She'd long ago accepted
his habit of accumulating odd items in his bedroom. After
her husband got sick, she'd been too busy to notice the slow
transformation of her house to a vast stockpile of potentially
valuable property. Lately, though, she'd been on him about
clearing it out—or moving out.

He found a seven-watt bulb, carried it outside, and
fitted it into a small wooden box with a tight-fitting lid.
The interior was painted black. One side had a small hole,

over which he'd fastened translucent red tape. A 110 electric wire ran from the box to a coil he'd rigged to a stationary bike. He set a stopwatch to time himself and rode for a while, checking to see if the red tape glowed. He knew it would take a while to build up the charge, and he rode faster, determined not to glance at the box and jinx the undertaking. It was boring and repetitious. His pants were too tight. He slowed the pumping of his legs and unsnapped his jeans, then pulled the zipper down. It was a little easier.

Jacky worked up a powerful sweat and felt as if his clothes were swimming on his body. His black-rimmed glasses were held in place by a shoelace tied to the arms. He heard a vehicle, then saw a police car stop at the yard. His cousin emerged from the car with a stranger.

"Hey, Cuz," Johnny Boy said. "Got a minute?"

Jacky shook his head to indicate no. The motion caused sweat to run into his eyes, and he began blinking, unable to see the black box.

"Is that red hole glowing?" he said.

"What?" Johnny Boy said.

"On the black box. Tell me if that red tape is lit up."

Johnny Boy followed the wire to the small box, surprised to see that a piece of red tape was indeed brighter than normal, as if illuminated from within.

"Sure is," he said.

Satisfied, Jacky lifted his feet from the pedals and stopped the watch. Eleven minutes. He wiped sweat from his eyes, slid off the bike, and bent over the box. He reset the watch and observed the tape.

"Got a feller here," Johnny Boy said, "wants to make a proposition to you."

The tape was slowly losing its glow. Jacky moved closer, concentrating. When the red color faded to its standard dullness, he stopped the watch. He stood upright, and his unsnapped pants began sliding down his hips. He grabbed them, but his undies had been briefly visible, and he glanced at the house, hoping his mother hadn't seen anything.

"You need you a belt, Cuz," Johnny Boy said.

"Eleven minutes of work for forty seconds of light. Not good enough."

He affixed his pants in place, slid the watch in his pocket, and wiped his face with his shirttail.

"You making your own electricity?" Mick said.

"Yup."

"If you geared down the bike, you might get more power out of it. Like those ten-speeds going up a hill. In Europe they've got some with twenty-seven speeds."

"Hmm. Must be using nine-speed drivetrains with three sets."

"That's right," Mick said. "They race them over there. Hills are bigger than ours."

"Might try that," Jacky said. "Right now, I've got a storage problem."

"Use a flywheel."

"Too heavy. I'm thinking hydro. A gravitational potential approach."

The screen door banged open on the porch, and Jacky's mother waved to Johnny Boy.

"Come say hi to your uncle," she said. "More than his own boy will do."

Johnny Boy nodded and walked toward the house.

"You're mechanical-minded?" Mick said to Jacky.

"I can take anything apart and make it better. That got boring so I started on my own work. Storing electricity right here lately. These old hills ain't fit for solar panels."

Mick nodded. Despite the bright sun, the woods on the western slopes were deeply shaded. Good for oaks and hickories, ginseng and morels, but not for capturing solar energy.

Jacky tugged his shirt away from his body and shivered from the cooling perspiration.

"What else you working on?" Mick said.

"Couple of things. One is a coat to make you invisible. The back has a camera on it facing behind. The front's got a screen. Live feed from what's behind you. Anybody seeing you coming would think you weren't there."

"What about the head? People will see it floating."

"That's the problem, all right," Jacky said. "Up in Canada they made an invisible cloak for the army."

"They don't have an army."

"Maybe they do, and the cloak's working."

Mick laughed.

"I'm not kidding," Jacky said. "They could have a phalanx of tanks sitting on the border behind that cloak, just waiting on the chance."

"Why would Canada attack us?"

"The Great Lakes, son. The water's going to dry up everywhere else."

"Uh-huh," Mick said. "What else you working on?"

"Perpetual motion. But it's tough. Friction gets me every time."

"You got a prototype?"

"I don't let nobody see it. Might steal it."

"If you don't let anybody see it, how will you get investors?"

"You an investor there, buddy?"

"No, I'm on medical leave from the army. But I did see a model of da Vinci's perpetual-motion machine in Italy."

"The one with marbles?"

"Yeah, in the Galileo Museum. It could go a long time, but he ran into the friction problem, too."

"With enough time, we all do. Gravity's even worse. That's why old people shrink. Gravity and friction kill us all."

"How about letting me see your machine?" Mick said. "I give you my word I won't steal your idea."

"No pictures either."

Mick nodded and followed Jacky into a building that appeared ramshackle on the outside but had been renovated into a surprisingly clean and bright shop. Table saw, drill stand, milling machines, wood and metal lathes, a couple of sanders. A workbench held portable power tools and a vise. Rows of hand tools hung from the walls, each with its outline drawn by a Sharpie to facilitate storage after use. A shop vac on wheels was tucked into a corner.

Jacky pointed proudly to a short set of interlocking stairs made of wood with a hand crank protruding from the side. On a step in the middle was a metal Slinky. Jacky set the Slinky in motion, tipping the top of the coiled spring so that it folded down to the next step. With his other hand, he began turning the hand crank, which moved the steps upward. It was essentially a miniature escalator. Jacky cranked at the same speed as the Slinky, which kept it in motion but never reaching the bottom. The sight of it gave Mick a joy unknown for months—a machine that did nothing but provide delight. The Slinky's metallic sound combined with the creak of the wooden steps to create a form of music.

"It's the second version," Jacky said. "Tried a paddle wheel and a creek, but the flow of water wasn't consistent."

"Are you an inventor," Mick said, "or an artist?"

"I don't know. What's the difference?"

Mick shrugged and asked if he could turn the handle.

A few minutes later, Johnny Boy entered, saddened by his uncle's state. Sturdy and strong throughout his life, Uncle Billy was now a pale lump beneath the blankets. His effort to breathe was laborious and often ended in a prolonged coughing that frightened Johnny Boy, as if his uncle might expel part of his ragged lungs. He'd worked as a coal miner for twenty years but was ineligible for federal black lung benefits. A new law made Kentucky the only state that blocked radiologists from evaluating X-ray images of damaged lungs. This benefited coal companies but not the dying workers.

Johnny Boy had stayed in his uncle's bedroom briefly and felt guilty for leaving. Encountering Mick playing with a Slinky was a sight as shocking as seeing his dying uncle. Mick stopped cranking the handle. The Slinky continued to the bottom of the steps, dropped to the floor, and traveled a little farther across the cement until losing momentum. They all watched it, then looked at each other.

"Any good with old cars?" Mick said to Jacky.

"Easy as *A-B-C*. Older is the easiest."

"How about a 1963 Stepside Chevy truck?"

"If you say 'Stepside,' I know it's a truck."

Mick nodded.

"What's in it?" Jacky said.

"One-forty horse. The 230 model. I need to get it running."

"What'll you pay?"

"Johnny Boy," Mick said. "What do mechanics around here get?"

"Twelve something an hour is what I give."

Mick looked at Jacky and waited.

"Naw," Jacky said. "I ain't like all them others."

"Twenty bucks an hour," Mick said. "No more."

"What color is it?"

"That old-timey blue with a white roof."

"Well, okay," Jacky said. "I'll work on a blue one."

"One thing," Johnny Boy said. "You'll need to stay at his place. Keep an eye on it."

"I don't know about that," Jacky said. "All my tools and stuff are here."

"How about this," Mick said. "We'll get somebody to haul in what you might need. You can always come back for supplies."

"Well," Jacky said, "I could use some private time for making designs. How far away is it?"

"About thirty-five minutes."

"When do you want me to start?"

"As soon as I get the road cleared. It's got a little overgrown."

"Rent me a mini-dozer," Jacky said, "and I'll do it."

"You can run one?"

"Dumber guys than me do it every day."

Mick and Jacky shook hands and nodded once to each other. In the hills such an agreement would hold until the job was done. They left the shed, and Jacky walked them to the county vehicle. He was preoccupied, as if already cataloging the materials he'd need to transport to the cabin.

"Hey, Cuz," Johnny Boy said. "What're the doctors saying about your dad?"

"Nothing good."

"Sorry to hear that. You ever think about inventing something to make some money?"

"Like what?"

"Like Big Mouth Billy Bass. Remember that?"

"A fake fish that turns its head and sings 'Take Me to the River.' After ten minutes, nobody liked it."

"It made a hundred million dollars in a year. I read an article about it on the internet."

"No, thanks. You can keep the internet. And your ideas, too."

"Johnny Boy," Mick said. "Can I use your cell phone? Need to call the mini-dozer people."

"Where's your phone?" Johnny Boy said.

"At Linda's house."

"A lot of people carry them around, you know."

Mick nodded.

"I don't have one," Jacky said. "They give you brain cancer."

Johnny Boy passed Mick his phone, then sat in the SUV, disgusted with the whole situation. His cousin was a known crackpot, and Mick had teamed up with him. Johnny Boy liked Big Mouth Billy Bass. He'd owned three in his life.

Mick joined him, and they drove back to Rocksalt. Johnny Boy was so irritated he forgot to wave to oncoming drivers.

"Why'd you offer him twenty bucks an hour?" he said.

"I think your cousin is some kind of genius."

"Because of that Slinky and a bunch of boards? That thing don't do a damn thing."

"Maybe that's the point."

Chapter Seven

Linda parked her Camry in front of a house with no near neighbors and honked the horn twice. Three boards embedded in the mud made a path between the road and the house. She checked the occupant's name against her list of property tax rolls and honked again. The curtains wiggled. The front door opened tentatively, and a man stepped onto the porch. Burly from the waist up, he had short, spindly legs that ended at unlaced work boots. Linda approached the house, staying on the lengths of lumber.

"Hidy, Mr. Campbell," she said. "I'm Linda Hardin. I'm running for sheriff."

"Ain't you already the sheriff?"

"Yes, sir, but I'm off duty now. That's why I'm in my own car. The election's coming up in a week, and I'm hoping you'll vote for me."

"Why?"

"I'm experienced. I've lived here all my life. I understand what people want and how to smooth problems out."

"What people want," Mr. Campbell said, "is to stay
out of jail."

"The sheriff's office doesn't have a jail. It's the county
one, in Rocksalt."

"Same thing, ain't it?"

"Yes and no. The city police and the judge lock people
up. Mainly, I settle disputes out here in the county."

"I get along with everybody."

"I'm glad to hear that," she said. "But you never know
when something might come up. A trespasser. Pack of dogs.
A neighbor running a meth lab. Even a disagreement over
a fence line. That's when I can help you."

"What do I get out of it?"

"You get a fair-minded person to listen to you."

She reached in her pocket for a brochure that included
a refrigerator magnet and a smaller business card proclaim-
ing her bona fides and accomplishments. He looked over
the material.

"Ain't you the one who arrested her own brother?"
he said.

"Yes, sir. He was AWOL from the US Army. I sent
him back under a federal warrant."

"Why'd you do that?"

"It's the law, Mr. Campbell. One thing you can trust,
I'll always be evenhanded with everybody."

He stared past her at her car, then watched a purple martin fly into a hollow gourd hanging from a tree limb. Linda followed his gaze to the gourd swaying from the weight of the bird's entrance.

"Do they really eat mosquitoes?" she said.

"Sure do. Other insects, too."

"You raise them gourds?"

"Yeah, I got a garden out back. Got butternut squash bigger than a small pig."

They looked toward the garden's location as if they could see through the house. Linda wondered how big a small pig was.

"My wife," the man said, "she's got a nephew I'd like to keep out of jail."

"Is he up to something you're worried about?"

"Might be."

"Are you scared of him?" she said.

"Naw, ain't like that. My wife's sister got carpal tunnel from that sewing factory in West Liberty. Can't work no more. Can't even weed her own garden. She likes to watch TV, but the regular shows bored her half to death. Her boy, he gets cable pumped into her house. It ain't on the up-and-up, but it's the only thing makes her happy. I don't want the law to make him stop. Then she'd be over here aggravating my wife."

"Your nephew," she said. "Does he bring cable TV into your house?"

"No, I can't abide no TV. Stupid people doing stupid things, and everybody thinks it's funny or takes it dead serious."

"Not even sports?"

"If the Reds are playing on free TV, I turn the sound down and listen to the radio. Those radio guys are a whole lot smarter than the TV people."

"My mom and I used to do that. She got the habit off her daddy."

"Well," he said. "It's a good way to do."

"If you ain't getting free cable," she said, "it's none of my business. If anybody was to complain about your sister-in-law, I'll take care of it. Keep your nephew out of jail."

"You promise?"

"Long as that's all he does, yes."

"Well," he said. "Hmm."

"I noticed you don't have a sign in your yard. Would you mind if I put one of mine up?"

"A voting poster on a stick?"

"Yes," she said. "Two sticks really, made of wire."

"In the grass out there's all right, I reckon."

"Thank you."

He turned to enter the house, and Linda went to her car. From the trunk she retrieved a vinyl campaign sign on metal rods, which she pounded into the soft earth with a ball-peen hammer. She still had ten more houses to visit today, but this one was the most important. Grady

Campbell was the oldest of the second generation of the family, which gave him the most influence. Linda had spoken to his mother earlier and won her over after an hour of listening to chitchat and gossip. The Campbells numbered forty-eight eligible voters, and she wanted them all. The fact that stealing cable signal was a federal crime, not within the sheriff's purview, gave sufficient cover for her white lie.

Two hours later Linda had placed the rest of the signs, gaining another eleven votes, and returned to town. At the sheriff's office she was pleased to see her SUV parked in its reserved spot. She walked around it, finding no dents or scrapes. She hoped Johnny Boy had remembered to move the driver's seat back. Though taller than Linda, he liked to drive hunched over the wheel for greater vigilance.

Sandra sat inside the door at her dispatcher's desk intent on her computer. She glanced up and shook her head, meaning no calls had come in and none pending. Mick stood in the cramped room that passed for Johnny Boy's office, looking at a sheaf of papers.

"Get any votes?" Johnny Boy said.

"Fifty to sixty," Linda said.

"It'll depend on the weather."

"I might drive them to the polls," she said. "Hire a van for the day. Find a driver."

"You do that, and they'll want to stop at stores."

"Ever what the people want," Linda said. "What are y'all looking at?"

"City file," Johnny Boy said. "Fuckin' Barney's murder. Made a copy for Mick."

Linda's faced clouded over like dropping a blackout curtain. She stared at her brother, gestured to her office, and left. Mick followed with the papers, wrinkled from a jam in the printer. He liked her office. Its squared-away quality reminded him of the military. Johnny Boy's was stiff as new jeans, the tidiness having crossed the line into compulsive rearranging.

"I saw that photograph on Johnny Boy's desk," Mick said.

"The one of me arresting you?"

"Yeah, he tipped it facedown, but he's about as sly as a blind puppy."

"It was in the Lexington paper, Ashland, and Carter County, too. Fact is, Big Bro, it's helping me get votes."

She sat behind her desk and he took the guest chair. He'd sat hundreds of times in a similar fashion before superior officers. That he faced his sister made no difference. He was proud of her, although he'd never tell her.

"I'm tired," she said. "Campaigning's not my strong suit. You walk today?"

"Seven miles."

"What are you doing with that city file?"

"Fuckin' Barney's mom asked me to look into it. She thinks there's more to it than the cops do."

"You and that family," she said. "I don't get it."

"Mrs. Kissick dated Dad in the old days."

"That doesn't mean a damn thing."

"If I can help her, I will."

"Don't you have enough to do helping yourself?"

"One doesn't rule out the other. Fuckin' Barney got shot down like a dog. The guy might kill somebody else. There's never just one. If I can stop it, I will. I had enough of people dying to last a lifetime."

She leaned back in the swivel chair and stared at the ceiling. Her brother never talked about his combat experience, but she knew it'd been pretty rough. Probably unimaginable. Despite being capable of violence, he operated from a base of compassion that surprised her. He didn't even kill insects, wouldn't poison ants. His way was to dig up two big hills, then dump the dirt from the first hill on the second, and vice versa. The ants fought it out, and the survivors moved elsewhere. Helping the Kissick family would keep him active and give her time alone at her own house.

"You going to investigate?" she said.

"Much as I can. I got some time left."

"Anything in the report?"

"Not much," he said. "Crime scene photos show packets of heroin on the ground beside him. Cops say it was a drug deal gone bad. But a customer would have taken them."

"So, you're suspicious?"

"Curious," he said.

"Don't go around aggravating anybody," she said. "I've got an election to win."

"Somebody's already pretty bad aggravated."

"Who's that?"

"Mrs. Kissick."

Linda acknowledged that fact with a signature combination of movements—closing her eyes for three seconds, shrugging, and issuing a soft sigh through pursed lips. The lack of profanity meant she was reluctantly resigned to things.

"Not many Kissicks," she said. "They mostly don't vote."

"They might if I help them. Can you ask Johnny Boy to run me back to your house?"

"Sure," she said. "But after that, he's done driving you around on the county dime."

"I'm getting my truck fixed."

"Is it worth it?"

"Probably not, but I like that truck. Johnny Boy's cousin is on it."

"Which one?"

"Jacky Turner. Know him?"

"Sure. Lives with his folks. Keen as a briar. Crazy as a soup sandwich."

Mick nodded and left. Ten minutes later, he stood in Linda's kitchen with his cell phone, calling a cab. He requested Albin, the man who'd found the dead body, and the dispatcher laughed. "Ain't nobody else but Albin driving today," he said. "He'll be there in five."

Mick's leg and hip hadn't bothered him all day. He wondered if it was the rehab finally paying off, or if the day's activities had taken his mind elsewhere. Either way he was grateful. He tucked his Beretta M9 into a leather holster at the small of his back under his shirt. He hadn't carried in weeks, and its weight was a familiar comfort.

The cab arrived, and he climbed into the back seat. Albin's hair was trimmed in the style of a mullet, not a full-blown Kentucky Waterfall, but something more subtle.

"Where to?" Albin said.

"Western Auto."

"That's been closed down ten years."

"Take me to the parking lot. You know where that's at?"

"Sure do," Albin said. "I'm the one found that dead feller there last week."

Mick nodded. The killer wouldn't have volunteered that information so readily. Still, Albin may have seen or heard something, a detail he didn't know was valuable. Albin cruised down Lyons to the cross street.

"Say you found the body," Mick said.

"Damn sure did."

"Did you get called there for a fare?"

"Naw. I was on break. Seen him laying there and thought maybe he needed a ride. You know, a drunk passed out or something."

"What'd you do?"

"Called the law. I drive a taxi, not an ambulance."

"How'd you know he was dead?"

"I never. But he didn't look good and had blood all over him."

Albin slowed on Second Street, then turned into the Western Auto lot, where a late-model Ford was idling. The young man behind the wheel glanced at the taxi and drove away immediately, accelerating on the blacktop. In the passenger seat a woman with long red hair looked out the back window.

"Know them?" Mick said.

"Nope. Kids been coming here a lot. You know, to see where a man died. If somebody's killed in a car wreck, they go look at the car."

"Do me a favor," Mick said. "Walk over there with me and let me see where you found him."

With the reluctance of a farmer dismounting his tractor, Albin left the cab. He stretched his back and rolled his shoulders.

"Where'd you park the night you found him?" Mick said.

"Right yonder beside what used to be the back door."

"If it was dark, how'd you see the body?"

"Headlights."

"Uh-huh. Show me exactly where he was laying."

Albin escorted him across the lot, which was in disrepair—crumbled tar, patches of gravel, patches of dirt. Fresh tire tracks from a number of vehicles marked the lot. Albin stopped and pointed.

"Right there," he said.

"Wait here a minute," Mick said.

He moved slowly in a lateral direction, making a ring around the area Albin had designated. Eyes intent on the ground, Mick gradually tightened the circle. A patch of bare earth held a curved line, and he looked for another one a few feet parallel—wheel tracks from the collapsible gurney on which the body had been loaded. Mick squatted and stared at the ground. No blood. No ejected cartridges. Nothing but a small section of earth on which a man had died.

He removed a copy of the crime scene photo, studied the background, and positioned himself where the photographer had stood. Barney was on his back, one arm under his body, the other stretched toward the lens. Mick had been in this situation many times—visiting the scene of violent death seeking insight and coming up with nothing.

He returned to Albin, who was humming a vague tune that sounded like garbled classic rock.

"Where were you before you pulled in here?" Mick said.

"Driving around, waiting on dispatch."

"Where'd you go?"

"Ain't that many places to go," Albin said. "Up and down Main Street, past the bars, but it was too early. Cruised the college. Then came here to wait."

"Why here?"

"I can get anywhere in town quick. At night it's shaded pretty good. I can take a nap if I've a mind to."

"Did you?"

"No, I seen the body before I could."

"Any other cars?"

"Probably passed a few driving."

"I mean here."

"No, nothing. Just me."

"Did you hear anything?"

"Like what?"

"Another car. People talking. A radio. Gunshots."

Albin rubbed the right side of his head, frowning in thought. He squinted and aimed his gaze up and to the right.

"No, can't say I did. And I would've. I had the windows down and no music."

Mick nodded, satisfied that he was telling the truth. The temporal lobe on the right side of the brain stored memory. When someone lied, they often looked left, to the creative part of the brain.

"I got one more place to go," Mick said. "You can keep the meter running and wait on me."

"Are you part of the family?" Albin said. "The Kissicks?"

"Naw, I'm helping them out is all."

Albin got in his car, slightly puzzled by the situation. The guy talked like a cop but wasn't one. As far as he knew, the Kissicks didn't have any friends, just customers. Nobody worked for them except family members. Maybe this short stranger was with the FBI. He could hook Albin up with the evasive-driving course.

Chapter Eight

Marquis Sledge III was a local undertaker who doubled as the Eldridge County coroner. His father and grandfather had performed the same job, burying the dead and assisting police, a legacy that went back fifty years. Lately Marquis had been concerned that his son wouldn't take over the business when the time came. Marquis blamed the internet. His three kids spent an inordinate amount of their daily life watching YouTube videos, especially fifteen-year-old Marquis IV. He wanted to be an "influencer," a term that puzzled his father.

With no impending funerals or viewings scheduled, Marquis had sent his receptionist home and begun preparing an order of supplies. Intent on his work, he was momentarily startled by the light tapping of someone at the door. He gathered himself, slipped on a dark suit coat of a plain style, and arranged an appropriately dolorous expression on his face—lessons learned from his father. He opened the door to the sheriff's brother. Marquis had known Mick vaguely in high school, then worked with him on a homicide case a year ago. He was one of the few people in the county who seemed utterly comfortable with Marquis despite his job.

Marquis welcomed him and offered a seat. His office was functional, with a photo of his family, two framed diplomas, and an award from the Kentucky Funeral Directors Association. A discreet machine in the corner purified the air, imbuing it with a slight fragrance of rosemary to cut any trace of embalming chemicals. Mick thought it smelled like roast chicken.

"Slow day?" Mick said.

"Slow season. There's more deaths in January. Then it tapers off."

"What about gun deaths?"

"Kentucky's in the middle. Texas has the most. Hawaii the least."

A piece of sunlight crept past the edge of the window and illuminated the far corner. The hillside behind the funeral home was dark from heavy shadow. A long slice of cloud drifted above the tree line.

"What's your interest in these stats?" Marquis said.

"Barney Kissick."

Marquis stood and opened a tan filing cabinet, withdrew a tan folder, and placed it on his desk, which had a tan desk pad. It was the old-time kind, a blotter with padded slots on the sides to hold paper. The office walls and curtains were tan, too. Marquis opened the folder and looked through his report.

"He had three gunshot wounds to the chest," he said. "One through-and-through. One hit a lung, resulting in pneumothorax."

He glanced at Mick, waiting for the inevitable request for translation of medical terminology.

"Collapsed lung," Mick said. "Third bullet?"

"Nicked the heart. Occlusion of the distal right coronary artery."

"Cause of death?"

"Acute blood loss."

Mick nodded. Marquis had confirmed the information that was included in the Rocksalt PD incident report.

"Did you examine the body at the scene?" Mick said.

"Yes," Marquis said. "Pronounced him, then did preliminary postmortem here."

"Was there blood at the scene, enough to indicate bleeding out?"

"No," Marquis said.

"Internal bleeding?"

"Very little."

"That's not in the police report."

"You're the only one who asked."

Mick nodded, thinking things through. Nobody had contacted Marquis because a known drug dealer was found shot to death in possession of heroin.

"Could he have been killed elsewhere," Mick said, "then moved?"

"I don't know. I'm not a policeman."

"Hypothetically," Mick said.

"Yes, it's possible that the body was moved postmortem."

"Highly possible?"

"If I were a policeman," Marquis said, "that would be a viable conclusion due to the lack of blood at the scene."

"Any evidence on the body?"

"No defensive wounds. He had clay dirt under his fingernails."

"There's clay everywhere in these hills."

"This was a significant amount. More clay than dirt."

"Like he was handling it?"

"I don't know what he was doing, but he'd had both hands in clay before he died."

Mick nodded, trying to piece it all together with not much luck. The local soil held enough clay to merit two brick manufacturing companies, both closed down long ago. There'd been at least one more over the county line, too.

"Are his personal effects here?" Mick said.

"The police took his phone, gun, wallet, the drugs, and a bullet lodged in his chest cavity. Hit a rib, then the sternum."

"What caliber?"

"It was beat up from bouncing around in him," Marquis said. "But my guess is a .45."

"Anything else?"

"The body didn't have a wristwatch or jewelry. I have the clothes."

"I'd like to see them. Do you mind?"

Marquis stood and left the room. Mick waited, studying the tan decor, wondering about its practical function. Hospital personnel began wearing aquamarine scrubs during surgical procedures because it was the color complement to the pink of body tissue. The combination reduced eye strain for a surgeon. The army used olive green for standard uniforms because the color faded into darkness faster than other hues. Tan must be related to dealing with grief.

Marquis returned carrying a large plastic bag. He carefully removed jeans, a shirt, and socks. Beside them he placed a pair of work boots. The knees of the jeans had yellowish residue, similar to the color of local clay. Mick examined the sole of each boot. The thick ridges were spaced a quarter inch apart and held plenty of dirt, some dark, some light.

"Who does forensic geology for you?" Mick said.

"State police, mainly. I can't make the request. It has to come from the investigating officers."

"What about private forensics?"

"Any results wouldn't be official."

"Neither am I," Mick said. "I'd like to take some dirt from a boot. That way if the case goes further, you'll have the other boot."

"Why?"

"If he was moved, maybe the dirt will indicate where he was killed. It's a long shot, but it's all I've got."

Marquis pondered a moment, then produced a small Ziploc bag. Mick used his pocketknife to carefully scrape all the dirt from the left boot into the bag. Marquis watched silently, and Mick waited, sensing that the man wanted to talk. He probably didn't have much chance for conversation here.

"Why is everything tan?" Mick said.

"My grandfather started the business in 1970. Back then the style for funeral homes was somber—heavy curtains, dark walls, and dark trim. I updated the interior with more windows and brighter carpets. Get some light in. I wanted my office to be uniform but not bland. Tan is warm and easy to match. Not as stark as all white. And not as depressing as Granddad's old way."

Something struck the exterior window with a thump. Mick set the bag of dirt on the desk, went outside, and circled the building. On the ground below the window lay a goldfinch. He carefully picked up the stunned bird, cradling it in one hand. The neck of the finch pulsated rapidly. Its eyes were open. Mick prodded it, and the wings gave a feeble flap. He lifted the bird to his mouth and gently blew into its open beak three times. The bird stood on his palm, breathing fast. It cocked its head to look at Mick, glanced about as if to get its bearings, then flew away.

Mick went back inside. Marquis was standing at the window looking out.

"That's the first time something came back to life here," Marquis said.

"Everything deserves another chance."

"Even Mr. Kissick?"

Mick nodded.

"Dr. Harker at the college," Marquis said. "She has an interest in soil forensics. And a lab."

Mick thanked him and left. He scanned the area for more finches guarding their territory and saw none. Albin was humming in the cab when Mick sat in the back.

"Where to now?" Albin said.

"The college. You know which one's the geology building?"

"Nope, but I can find it. You sure about this? I'll have to keep the meter running."

"Yeah," Mick said. "I have a proposition for you. My truck's broke down for a few days. How about I hire you as my driver?"

"Private?"

Mick nodded.

"I'll have to check with dispatch," Albin said.

"Drop me off first."

Rocksalt State had begun as a normal school to produce teachers for the hills, then expanded into a college. It was known as a "suitcase school" because the majority of students went home on the weekends. Hill culture mandated fierce family loyalty and a generalized suspicion of education. Young people needed to reassure their families that they hadn't gotten above their raisings due to the pernicious influence of the classroom. Many parents feared that their kids would get a degree and move away for work, leaving them to get old alone.

Originally laid out with interconnecting lanes, the college had recently closed a few streets to traffic, which made the campus more amenable to students on foot. Conventional GPS was still trying to catch up with modernity, and Albin made a few false starts, encountering deadends and one-way streets before he found a tight alley off Main Street that led to the geology building.

Mick left the car and walked to Glasser Hall, built in 1937 of red brick with granite trim. The front had sixty-four windows, giving it the appearance of urban factories built in the nineteenth century. He crossed the broad yard to the main entrance. Classes were in session, which left the halls relatively empty, and he was able to find the geology department easily. A receptionist informed him that Dr. Harker was in class for another twenty-three minutes. Mick waited, appreciating the precision of the designated time. He read a brochure and learned that the correct name was "earth science," not "geology." He supposed the term made it more attractive to undergraduates. Mick's own college education had taken nine years and spanned three countries while serving in the military. A degree was necessary for promotion to the Criminal Investigation Division, a goal he'd set when he became weary of parachuting into combat zones.

Two young men walked by staring at their phones. They could have been fresh recruits out of boot camp. Three women strolled the other direction, capturing the attention of the men, and Mick wondered how his life might have been if he'd stayed in Eldridge County and gone to college here. He'd be the same age, of course, quite possibly divorced, but his body wouldn't bear scars from bullet, knife, and shrapnel.

He went to Dr. Harker's office and stood by the locked door. She arrived shortly, trailed by two students who clearly adored her. She offered encouragement and reminded them about an extra-credit seminar. Dr. Harker was short, energetic, and quick on her feet. She wore a pair of men's trousers from a 1940s-era suit, complete with sharp creases, two-inch cuffs, and a subtle plaid. She smiled at Mick with genuine enthusiasm.

"Waiting for me?" she said.

Mick nodded. She unlocked her office and invited him in. The small room held a wall of bookshelves, desk, chair, computer, and guest chair. The rest of the furniture functioned as surfaces upon which was heaped a startling array of disorganized material. Books, papers, and stacks of spiral notebooks leaned against four piles of standard blue books. On a shelf was a bobblehead figure holding a shovel, with a small photo of Dr. Harker glued to the face. The walls held topographic maps and indecipherable soil charts. Mick was pleasantly surprised to see that the room lacked the standard row of framed diplomas. He'd never trusted people who displayed evidence of their accomplishments.

Dr. Harker settled into her chair, leaning back with an open posture, her eyes bright and merry behind small metal spectacles. Mick had consulted with academic personnel before but only in Europe, which had a decidedly different style of professor. He nodded to her.

"Marquis called," she said. "Said to listen to you. I'm listening. This is my listening face."

She smiled again, and Mick quickly filled her in on the situation and what he wanted.

"Do you have the mysterious bag o' dirt?" she said.

Mick passed it to her.

"Tell me," she said. "Are you up to no good?"

"No, ma'am. It's on the level. I'm helping the family."

"Did you go to school here?"

"No, ma'am. I joined the army eighteen years ago. Got my degree along the way."

"What do you want to know about this soil?"

"Anything," he said.

"Soil is informative," she said. "The earth tells all. Humans came out of water, migrated to land, and go back to the earth at death. All of human history is in that bag."

"Well," he said, "I don't really need all that. Ideally you could tell me where it came from. Or point me in the right direction."

"You don't want a history lesson on soil?"

"No, ma'am, not really."

She laughed, then leaned forward with elbows on her desk, her forearms taut with muscle.

"Good," she said. "If you had, I'd have politely declined. I'll examine this sample as a favor to Marquis. Come back in a week."

"Thank you, but I don't have that much time."

"I was afraid of that. How about two days?"

He stood and offered a hand. They shook once, a brief motion that reminded him of a French person meeting an American.

"Same time?" he said.

"No, three o'clock is better. It's quiet then, and I'll be waiting on my wife to pick me up."

Mick nodded and left. While closing the door he glimpsed Dr. Harker holding the Ziploc bag close to her face, peering at the contents. He walked through the halls, weaving among students dressed identically in sweatpants, garish sneakers, and oversize T-shirts bearing large Greek letters. Most of the males wore hats reversed on their heads, which defeated the purpose of the brim, unless it kept rain out of their collars. Albin's mullet would work just as well.

Albin's window was rolled down, and he stared longingly at a pair of female students strolling by. Each had a single earbud in place, the cords merging and plugged into a cell phone, allowing them to share the music. Mick envied their innocence. He climbed in the back seat.

"What'd dispatch say?" Mick said.

"They'll get someone to cover my shifts as long as you need me. How long you think it might be?"

"It's untelling," Mick said. "You know where the Kissick place is?"

"Sure do. I went to school with Mason."

"Let's go."

"Are we in a hurry?"

Mick heard a hopeful tone in Albin's voice. It surprised him because most cabbies preferred a slow pace in order to maximize the fare. Maybe Albin had a date, or an appointment with his barber.

"Yeah, man," Mick said. "The faster the better."

Chapter Nine

Albin drove slowly down Normal Avenue to Main Street and turned onto a street that emptied into the new bypass. He headed east, merging with US 60. At the city limits he pressed the accelerator to the floor. The V-6 engine roared, and the car hit fifty miles per hour in five seconds before he had to slow for the first curve. He reached seventy on a short straight section, braked before a sharp curve and accelerated into it. The road opened to a two-mile straight stretch with three hills. Albin kept the gas pedal to the floor and touched ninety, then slowed for a series of hard curves. He reached Big Perry Road in five minutes, a new personal best. There was one more straightaway before he had to reduce his speed and turn onto the narrow lane toward the Kissick home place.

He relaxed and glanced at Mick in the rearview mirror.

"Fast enough for you?" Albin said.

"Don't you worry about the law?"

"Naw, I know where they set up at. Besides, I figure an FBI guy like you would get me out of a jam."

"I ain't in the FBI," Mick said. "I'm in the army."

"Shit. That sucks."

Mick nodded. The boy was an impressive driver and didn't talk as much as Johnny Boy. Albin parked on the side of the road beside the Kissick house.

"Wait here," Mick said.

He walked across the yard, climbed the steps, and knocked on the door. Mason opened it.

"Is that Albin out there?" he said.

Mick nodded, and Mason walked to the car with a big smile.

Shifty Kissick sat in the same chair she'd occupied on his last visit, watching television with no volume. Mick remained standing until she gestured to a chair.

"Find out who killed my boy?" she said.

"No, ma'am. I got the police report. There's some pictures I want to show you."

"I don't want to see none of Barney."

"They're not him, Mrs. Kissick. It's what he had on him."

He passed her four photographs of the wrinkled glassine bags containing heroin. Two were close-ups of a yellow crown stamped on the packet.

"They ain't his," she said. "Damn sure not."

"How can you tell?"

"Do you know anything about this business?"

"No, ma'am. Nothing."

"Way it works, everybody's got a little picture they put on their bags, like advertising. Barney's was a blue star. This yellow crown means it was somebody else's."

"Another dealer's heroin, you mean?"

"Yes, not Barney."

"Who uses a yellow crown?" he said.

"I don't know."

"Where'd the blue star come from on the bags?"

"Mason stamped them."

"Could he have made a mistake? Put the wrong picture on the bags?"

"He only had the one stamp. If he did it wrong, Barney would have seen it. He checked them all."

"Any reason Barney might've used another stamp? The yellow crown?"

"No, he was proud of the blue star. Everybody knew it was his. Good stuff out of Detroit. He called it branding."

"Who else sells heroin around here?"

"I can't talk about that. Is this all the far you got? Some pictures of dope that ain't even his?"

"It's a start, Mrs. Kissick. I told you I'd look into it and see if it was worth continuing."

"Is it?"

"Yes, ma'am, I believe so. Something's not right. I'm trying to figure out what exactly. Knowing who sells the yellow crown will help me."

"What do you aim on doing?"

"Got a few ideas."

"I need to know."

"Ma'am," Mick said, "I ain't working for you and I don't answer to you."

"Then who the hell are you working for?"

"People who ain't been killed yet."

Her shoulders slumped, and she closed her eyes. He waited. Last year Shifty would have run him off with a gun, but she was weaker now. He was careful not to move or blink. He watched her struggle, then acquiesce to practicality.

"There's a bunch up Christy Creek," she said. "Way past old Hogtown in Elliott County. Barney went up there and worked out some kind of deal. I don't know what it was. Rich Lange, his two boys, and a married-in. They started with weed, then pills. Pretty rough folks. Rich, he'd drown you in your own well."

Mick nodded and went outside. Mason was leaning on the car door, laughing with Albin. Mick heard the tail end of an anecdote involving an aerial drone and a Roomba, something about sending them into battle. They hushed at Mick's approach.

"Mason," Mick said, "your mom says you stamped the heroin."

"Yep."

"What did you use?"

"A rubber thing carved with a star. The ink was blue."

"You ever use another stamp?"

"Ain't got but that one."

Mick showed him the photographs.

"Looks like bottle caps."

"They're upside down, Mason."

Mason inverted the photographs and grinned.

"Crowns!"

"You know them?"

"I never seen none but Barney's. They were plain till I put the star on them. It was fun doing that."

Mick nodded. He walked around the car and climbed in the passenger side beside Albin, who shifted gears and revved the engine. Mason stepped away, waving as if to a mail carrier bringing a long-expected letter.

"The back seat is safer," Albin said.

"I'd rather be up front. Easier to see when you're going to speed up or brake."

"Where to?"

"Up past old Hogtown to Elliott County."

"We in a rush?"

"No, I need to think about things a minute. You know the Langes up there?"

"I don't want to. They ain't to be fooled with."

"You can stay in the car."

Albin turned around and headed back the way they had come. He took the Haldeman Road past the remnants of the grade school Mick had attended, now resembling the ruin of an ancient fort. Albin drove up Open Fork to the top of the ridge, passing New Sill Cemetery and a smaller one occupied by a single family. Three crows lifted awkwardly from a ditch and settled on a sugar maple. The narrow blacktop descended in a series of curves to Route 32 past a church and the Ashley Fly Beauty Salon.

Albin turned onto a dirt road that climbed out of the holler to a high ridge. The woods were pressed solid along the road, with no ditches or wide areas to turn around. He stopped at the top in front of two signs that read NO TRESPASSING.

"What now?" Albin said.

"Go slow till we see somebody. Let me do the talking."

Albin eased the car forward sixty feet. A man stepped from the woods holding an AR-15 rifle. He wore jeans, a flannel shirt, and work boots. His head was a mess of cowlicks.

Albin stopped and Mick stepped slowly out of the car, both hands high and visible. He held the pistol by the trigger guard between his thumb and forefinger, the barrel aimed at the ground. The man lifted the AR-15. Mick placed his gun and phone on the hood of the car and moved out of reach.

"I'm Jimmy Hardin's boy, Mick."

"Says he's Mick Hardin."

Mick realized he was speaking into a cell phone strung around his neck on a homemade harness. He occasionally tilted his chin down as if aiming his voice at the phone. The rifle never wavered, aimed at Mick's center mass.

"What're you doing up here?" the man said.

"Talk to Mr. Lange. I'm a friend of Shifty Kissick."

The man relayed the information. The entire conversation had a stilted quality that reminded Mick of phone calls to his ex-wife on army phones from the Middle East. A several-second delay ensued between each person speaking.

"About what?" the man said.

"Fuckin' Barney."

"You a cop?"

"No."

"Daddy wants to know what you want."

"That's for him only."

There was a longer wait while the person on the other end of the phone thought this over. Mick stood calmly. A speckled wood thrush landed on the ground beside an ant hill constructed of loose earth. It plucked a couple of ants in its beak and rubbed them on its feathers. Mick hadn't seen that in a long time, since his grandfather pointed out the odd behavior. The bird flew to a fringe tree, its weight causing the slim branch to shift, then began its song.

"All right," the man said. "Come on, then."

Mick walked up the road. He could hear the man's heavy boots following, not a good trait for a sentry. He tucked the information away. At the top of the ridge two vehicles came into view at a fork—the road one way, a footpath in the other direction. Mick stopped.

"Go right," the man said behind him.

They followed the path around a heavy stand of cedar to a house with a wood-lap exterior and a broad-roofed porch. The tip of a flue beyond the roofline suggested an addition in the back. Another young man on the porch held a shotgun loosely and carried a holstered revolver. He spoke into a cell phone slung around his neck, high on his chest beneath his chin. Mick supposed he didn't hear that well.

The door opened behind him, releasing an older man who resembled the two guards mainly through the head hair. All three had the same cowlick on the left, two more on the right, and a whorl on the crown as if an entire herd had licked their heads. The older man's hair was solid gray.

"Say you're a Hardin," he said.

Mick nodded.

"You the one got arrested by his sister in Eldridge County?"

Mick nodded. The younger son on the porch grinned.

"Going to vote for her?" the older man said.

"Probably," Mick said. "If she don't lock me up again."

"What are you up here for?"

"Are you Mr. Lange?"

"Been a long time since a man called me that. I'm Rich."

"Shifty Kissick said to talk to you."

"What about?"

"Her boy getting killed."

"Fuckin' Barney," Rich said. "Nobody up here did it."

"I believe you," Mick said. "I got some pictures I'd like to show you. Mrs. Kissick seen them already."

"What kind of pictures?"

"Photographs. From when he got shot."

"That's all you want? Me to look at some pictures? What's in it for me?"

"Nothing," Mick said.

Rich grunted as if momentarily mirthful, then nodded at his son. The younger brother stepped off the porch, took the file of photos from Mick, and carried them to his father. Rich flipped through them quickly, then again at a slower pace.

"Where'd you get these?"

"My sister's deputy. They were on Fuckin' Barney when he got killed. Mrs. Kissick never seen them before either. Or Mason."

"That boy's a dam missing a river."

Mick nodded. They all stood for a minute watching one another as if it was part of each man's job. A breeze carried the faint scent of forsythia from the tree line. Mick sniffed the air.

"Late for forsythia," he said.

"It don't get the sun much," Rich said.

"Is that yellow crown your mark?" Mick said.

Rich jerked his head to his sons.

"Run get one."

The older one jerked his head to the younger one, who grimaced, stepped off the porch, and went around the house. Mick watched the shade retreat as the sun came farther above the hill. The land was quiet.

"No dogs?" Mick said.

"They know not to bark. And when to tear a man's leg off. You always travel by cab?"

"Truck's broke down. Albin knew the way, but he's too scared to leave the car."

"And you ain't?" Rich said. "Why's that?"

"No reason to be. I ain't against you."

Rich's son returned, and Rich motioned him to Mick. The packet was the same folded over glassine as the others, but this one had a bright red *R* imprinted on it.

"That's mine," Rich said. "I like the Cincinnati Reds."

"They ain't doing too good," the older son said. "I like the Cards."

Rich ignored him, so Mick did, too. He gave the packet to the young man, who dutifully returned to the porch.

"Mrs. Kissick said you and Barney had a deal. Some kind of split over who sold where. Eldridge County and Elliott County."

"I don't remember."

"Reckon somebody's trying to muscle in?"

"Maybe," Rich said. "Fuckin' Barney dead leaves a hole to fill."

"None of my business," Mick said. "Unless that's why he got killed."

"Wasn't us. And I don't know that yellow crown."

"I thank you for your time, Mr. Lange."

Mick nodded to each man and walked back to the car. His gun and phone were missing from the hood. Albin had tipped the seat back as far as it would go and was peeping through the bottom of the window. It was rolled halfway down.

"You got my gun in there?" Mick said.

Albin nodded. Mick circled the car and climbed into the passenger seat. Albin had already cranked his seat up and rolled down the window. He gave Mick his possessions.

"Let me guess," Mick said. "You figured if you heard gunshots you'd have to leave fast, and you were afraid my stuff would fall off the car."

"Sorry, man."

"Don't be. It's the smart thing to do."

"Where to?"

"Back to my sister's house where you picked me up. No rush."

Chapter Ten

By ten-thirty the next morning, Linda had placed eight signs and gathered fourteen votes. She'd also sweated through her uniform and discarded the official hat. It was too early to be this hot—too early in spring and too early in the day—and the politicians were fighting over climate change. If any of them went out and did a single day of work, they'd know a thing or two. She was hungry, but it was too soon for lunch.

Linda sat in her car with the air conditioner running and wondered if being sheriff was worth the aggravation. She made a mental list of the pros and cons, intending to tally up the amounts against each other, but by the time she finished the cons, she'd forgotten the number of pros. She searched the glove box and found a pen that advertised Sledge Funeral Home and wrote on a receipt from the IGA.

Pros:

    Free car

    State benefits

    Role model for girls

    Community status

    Helping people

Cons:

    Campaigning

    Bad hours

    Testifying in court

She studied the list and crossed out "Community status," because it didn't amount to more than some people being overly polite while others avoided her. Still, the pros outweighed the cons, which irritated her. She could add more cons, but that meant focusing on the negative, something she tried not to do. It really came down to campaigning, and she wrote it again under cons. Now the list evened out, four and four. She considered writing it again to make the cons longer. Then she realized her list was its own campaign against campaigning.

The Motorola built into the dashboard flashed, then emitted a buzzing sound. Linda clicked on the microphone. The dispatcher's voice crackled into the car.

"Base to Sheriff, come in."

"I'm here, Sandra."

"We got a dog emergency."

"Send Johnny Boy."

"He's at the other end of the county on a call. The dog emergency is somewhere on Tater Lick Road. Close to your location."

"What's the problem?" Linda said.

"Unknown."

"I never heard of a dog emergency."

"No, ma'am."

"Hope it's not rabies."

Linda wrote the details on the bottom of the IGA receipt, turned around, and headed back down Cranston Road. She slowed at the cemetery and waved to three older men tidying the graves. Nobody named Cranston lived in the county, and she wondered who the road was named for. Probably somebody in the Cranston Cemetery, maybe a whole family's worth. Johnny Boy would know.

The dog emergency was not on Tater Lick Road but back north along Tater Lick Branch, which was a section of Triplett Creek. After several attempts and two calls to dispatch, Linda found the correct house on Barn Branch Road, although there was no such name for the creek or family, and no barn in sight.

The house had lap siding painted light blue and trimmed in dark blue. It belonged to Stell Combs, short for Stella. She was sitting on her front porch staring at a fully leafed-out sugar maple beside the house. Linda parked and disembarked, adjusting her equipment belt for quick access to her pistol, in case the dog appeared rabid. She walked up the flagstones to the large porch. Stell wore a blue dress and a blue sweater, and her gray hair was pulled tight by a network of blue barrettes.

"Mrs. Combs," Linda said. "I'm Linda Hardin."

"I didn't expect the sheriff herself!"

"Yes, ma'am. Are you all right?"

"Oh, yes, I'm doing dandy. It's Skippy that's got the problem."

"Your dog emergency? Is he walking funny? Disoriented? Or hurt?"

"I don't know if he's hurt. He's stuck in that tree."

She pointed to the maple, and Linda wondered if Mrs. Combs was around the bend. Even so, Linda had to show due diligence.

"Been up there going on an hour," Stell said.

Linda circled the tree, looking up. It was an old maple, maybe eighty feet tall, with a large thermometer nailed to the trunk. She saw no dog and heard no dog. On the ground was a full bowl of dog food.

"Skippy!" Mrs. Combs called from the porch. "Skippy!"

Linda stepped back to view the upper boughs. A slight breeze cooled her face, rising to a gust. The leaves shifted position momentarily, and through a gap she briefly glimpsed a wisp of white fur about fifteen feet up. When the wind stopped, the fur vanished among the leaves, and she wondered if she'd imagined it. The fur might have been part of a bird's nest. Either way, she was grateful for the cooling wind.

She went to the porch and sat beside Stell in a wicker chair, white originally and repainted in blue, now a mottled weaving of willow plaits that leaked chips of pigment.

"Mrs. Combs," Linda said, "how'd your dog get in that tree?"

"It was the darnedest thing. I had all the windows and doors open for air, front and back. It's the first warm day of the year. It gets stuffy of the night, and I like to breathe."

Linda gave an "mm-hmm" in agreement that breathing was a good idea.

"Well," Stell continued, "Little Joey is outdoors mostly and—"

"Little Joey?" Linda said.

"The cat. A pretty good mouser. She plays heck on the moles, too. Little Joey was outside, and Skippy got after her. You know how dogs and cats are."

"Mm-hmm."

"Little Joey ran in the house, something she knows not to do, but it's springtime, and they get frisky. She ran up the stairs with Skippy chasing. Little Joey ran into my daughter's old bedroom, jumped out the window, landed on the porch roof, then jumped in the tree, with Skippy right behind her. Little Joey came straight down the tree, but Skippy stayed up in there."

"How do you know all this?"

"I was setting right here drinking coffee when it happened. Saw it all plain as day. Do you have a cigarette?"

"No, ma'am," Linda said. "I don't smoke."

"I don't either. But I ran out of nerve pills, and Skippy's stuck in a tree."

"Do you have a ladder?"

"I did but not no more. I lent it to Silas Henderson down the road. He died before giving it back, and I didn't have the heart to ask his kids for it. For all they knew, I didn't loan it to him and was trying to steal if off them."

"When was this?"

"Fourteen, fifteen years ago. They sold that house off. Maybe the ladder, too."

"Any family close?"

"I got seven daughters, but none live on Barn Branch. Three in town, one all the way over in Clearfield, two up Christy Creek. The youngest is out Flemingsburg Road. You know where that's at?"

"Yes, ma'am. It's on the way to Flemingsburg."

"Oh, yes. I knew that."

"Are your girls married?"

"Every one of them. I've got eleven grandbabies that I don't see enough of. The cutest little babies you ever did see. Four of them are in school."

She began listing the grades of each child, and Linda returned to her vehicle, doing math. With spouses, there were at least fifteen potential votes in exchange for helping a dog depart a tree. She radioed Sandra and asked if Johnny Boy was available to bring her a ladder.

"Not at the present, no. He's down at the Starkey Boat Ramp investigating graffiti."

"There's nothing to write on down there."

"Evidently they've got a little building now."

Linda released the speaker button. Starkey Boat Ramp was thirty miles away. Even if Johnny Boy were free, he'd be more than an hour getting here, plus finding a ladder on the way. A few months ago she'd dated Shane Tackett, but asking him for help meant he'd want something in return, as all men did. Then he'd complain that they didn't see each other often enough. If she pointed out that they could when he brought the ladder, he'd get mad. Linda was not up for either scenario. Her best option was her brother, who owed her for room, board, and the occasional shower.

Thirty minutes later, Linda sat on the porch, having just finished a lunch that Mrs. Combs had offered her—cheese and baloney on light bread with blueberries. It was apparently her specialty, the meal she'd routinely fed her daughters. Linda had written down their names with the intention of placing a sign in each of their yards. During the entire time, Mrs. Combs did not stop talking. If Linda tried to add a comment or seek clarification, Mrs. Combs simply raised her voice and continued her monologue as if talking above the sound of a sudden rain on a metal roof. Linda felt fatigued from listening and understood why the daughters had moved away and didn't visit.

Albin's cab drove into the yard with an aluminum extension ladder sticking out of the trunk. A T-shirt tied to the last rung served as a warning to traffic. Linda excused herself eagerly and crossed the grass to meet Mick. He was carrying a hank of rope slung over his shoulder.

"Hidy, Sis," he said. "At your service."

"A first for everything."

"Where's the dog?"

"Up that maple."

"Must've jumped off the porch roof. Was it chasing something?"

"How would you know something like that?"

"Window's open," Mick said. "What's the dog's name?"

"Skippy."

Mick carried the ladder to the tree and examined the ground and the bark. Staring up into the leaves, he walked around the maple, calling to the dog. He made another circuit, then went to the car.

"Albin," he said, "go talk to that lady. Ask for a drink of water or tell her you have to use the bathroom. Keep her in the house till we're done."

"Shouldn't be hard," Linda said. "She talks like a meth head."

Albin left the car and joined Mrs. Combs. Mick watched them enter the house.

"Why do you want her gone?" Linda said.

"A scared dog drools. There's none on the ground or bark. I can't hear any whimpering or whining."

"Maybe she's crazy and the dog's not up there. Maybe there never was a Skippy."

Mick tied the rope to his belt and raised the extension to the bottom of the first limb. He began climbing, one rung at a time, calling to the dog. Linda watched his torso slowly rise into the foliage. Through the swaying leaves she could see patches of his chambray shirt. The relentless voice of Mrs. Combs issued from the house, delivering a monologue on the history of the road beside her land—when it was initially paved, how often it was maintained, the location of two blind curves, and details of several minor accidents in the past few decades. Albin was silent throughout.

Leaves rustled in the maple. Descending slowly came a dog fastened to the rope by two loops. The head lolled at an unnatural angle, displaying a white-and-merle face. Skippy gently settled to the earth as if he'd lowered himself to a sleeping position. The rope fell through the leaves, making a loose pile beside the food bowl. Mick climbed down the ladder, and they looked at the dog, dirty white trimmed in brown, like an old station wagon.

"He was up there dead all this time?" Linda said.

"Broke his neck. His head was stuck in the third fork up."

"Shit fire and save matches," Linda said. "I still yet need her family's votes."

"Is that what this is about?"

"No. It was an official call."

"Dog in a tree. What's that on the ten code?"

"Fuck you, Big Bro," Linda said. "I got to go break the news. Worst part of this job is a death notification."

She went to the house and knocked on the door. Stell and Albin came outside. He was using a blue spoon to eat from a blue plastic bowl, and Linda wondered if everything she owned was the same color. Stell descended to the bottom porch step and stopped.

"Skippy didn't make it," Linda said.

"He died happy," Stell said. "Doing what he liked best. Chasing Little Joey."

"We can bury him, if you'd like us to."

"Thank ye, no," Stell said. "I'll wait and do it with my grandchildren. If they won't come here for a family funeral, I'll know the reason why."

Albin finished his snack, carried the empty bowl into the house, and returned. In his absence, Linda glanced between the dog and Stella, then stared at a decorative fence at the edge of the property. A red-winged blackbird landed on the top rail, gazed at the people, then moved on. Linda wished she could join the bird, fly away, and forget the circumstances.

"Mrs. Combs," Linda said. "Would you like us to put Skippy somewhere, so he's not in the yard?"

"There's a shed out back," Stell said. "Anywhere in there's fine. It'll keep the crows off him. I'm going to rest now. You'uns are welcome to stay."

Stell went inside. Mick carried the dog around the house, followed by Linda and Albin. He deposited the dog on an old workbench littered with rusty tools and the shed skin of a snake. They returned to the front. Mick put the ladder in the taxi's trunk.

"What were you eating?" Linda said to Albin.

"Blue Jell-O. She makes it for her grandkids, but they don't like it."

"Maybe because it's blue," Linda said.

"Everything in her kitchen is blue—curtains, table-cloth, cabinets, dishes, linoleum. Countertops, too. It was like standing inside the sky."

The three of them contemplated this information while a robin perched in the maple and contemplated them. A puff of breeze carried the scent of viburnum.

"We need to talk, Mick," Linda said. "Private. I'll give you a ride."

Mick nodded.

"Don't worry, Albin," he said. "I'll pay you for the full day. Drop that ladder at my sister's house."

Linda climbed behind the wheel of her SUV and watched her brother open the passenger door, pivot on his bad leg, and vault in.

"Looks like you're doing better," she said.

"Better than Skippy."

They drove in silence for a few miles. The western hills were darker green than the eastern slopes.

"I heard from Peggy," Linda said. "She knows you're in."

Mick nodded.

"Two texts and a voice mail," she said.

Mick nodded, waiting. Whatever it was, it wasn't good.

"She wants to get married," Linda said. "To that guy in Owingsville. She wants you to sign the divorce papers. You can mail them, or she'll pick them up."

"How'd she sound?"

"If you want to know, go see her. I'm done being the go-between. I told her that, too."

Mick nodded. While flying on Percocet he'd deleted Peggy's voice mail and texts, then forgotten about them. He didn't want to be divorced, but he didn't want to stand in the way of her life. He still loved her and always would. The baby was a year old. Marrying the father was for the best.

To distract himself, Mick looked through one of Linda's expensive election brochures, the tri-fold kind with glossy color photographs. It listed her accomplishments, which included solving the murders of Nonnie Johnson and Delmer Collins a year ago. Mick had given her pertinent information for both homicides.

"Nice work on Nonnie," he said.

"Between that and arresting you, people started liking me more as sheriff."

"The mayor and judge and them?"

"Yep, all the bigwigs. Murvil Knox, too. He paid for those fancy pamphlets and the signs."

"Do you trust Knox?" he said.

"Not one bit. All those big coal operators lie like a rug. Coal ain't coming back no matter what the politicians say. He's getting sued over mountaintop removal. There's people who lost their homes from landslides."

"But you'll take his money."

"It's not a whole lot, but yes. Don't you say a word about it being blood money either."

"He's probably funding your opponent, too."

They rode in silence for a few miles, past a family cemetery and a fenced-off section of terrain for cattle. Linda stopped twice at turnoffs, and Mick pounded signs into the shoulder of the road. At the T intersection where the road met Big Perry, he positioned Linda's signs for the best visibility in all three directions. She stopped at several houses and spoke to the occupants while he waited in the car. Twice he tried calling Jacky Turner but got no reception.

"You find out who killed Fuckin' Barney yet?" she said.

"No, not even close. One thing though, that heroin he had on him wasn't his."

"How do you know something like that?"

"These dealers, they mark the bags. It wasn't his mark."

"He's not the only guy selling," she said.

"No, he's not. I talked to his rival. Not his bag either. And nobody knows whose it is. A yellow crown. Whoever killed Fuckin' Barney put that heroin on him to make it look like a drug deal. But they made a mistake. It's not from around here."

"You sure about this?"

Mick nodded.

"Do I want to know how you got all this?"

"Best not, Sis."

She stared at the road for a mile, thinking things through.

"I got a buddy in the Lexington PD," she said. "I'll text him photos of the bags. Maybe he'll recognize the yellow crown."

"Good idea. Tell him it's not local."

"Don't tell me how to do my fucking job."

"Sorry, Sis."

"You're just spinning your wheels till the medical leave is up. Something to fill time, right? Keep your mind out of Owingsville."

Mick nodded.

"What are you going to do about your place?" she said.

"Which one?"

"In town. I know you love Papaw's cabin too much to get rid of."

"Give it to Peggy, but I don't want to clear it out."

"Too sad?"

Mick nodded. He tended to ignore his emotions, a habit that had kept him alive in war zones. Confronting how he felt made him vulnerable, another emotion he preferred to avoid.

"How about this," Linda said. "You and me go over there and box up what you want."

"I don't want anything."

"Family photographs? You might want one in a few years."

"You can have them."

"You haven't thrown much thought at this, have you?"

"No, I've been thinking about Fuckin' Barney. I believe he got killed somewhere else, then dumped in town. If he died outside the city limits, it's your jurisdiction."

"Shit, hell, damn it," she said. "I don't need that while running for office."

"Might push you into a win."

"Or I'll be the incumbent who couldn't catch the killer. What the fuck, Mick!"

"Your mouth will cost you more votes than that."

"I don't cuss except around you."

Mick nodded. His grandfather and great-grandfather had taught him everything they knew about the woods. Linda, they'd taught to cuss like a sailor. Blue language, the old men called it. Mick chuckled at the memory.

"What's so damn funny?" Linda said.

"Nothing. You take care of my house, and I'll look into Fuckin' Barney."

"Ain't that cussing, too?"

"Not if it's his name, no. If you talk to his mom, remember to just say Barney. She wants everybody to call him that now."

"You're kidding."

"Nope. It's like a promotion after death. A post-humous medal."

"You're too close to that family," Linda said. "Are they paying you?"

"Mrs. Kissick offered to. But I can't take her money."

"You don't make any sense. Two houses you ain't living in and working for free."

"Good point, Sis. Maybe I should run for sheriff. What's the story on the other guy?"

"Gerald Fisher. Older than me. Four years with the campus police and five years with the city force. Good family. People like him."

"Why'd he leave the city police?"

"A little fuzzy there. The mayor appointed a new chief, and Gerald left. The story is they didn't see eye to eye. You know how men are."

"You think it's something else?"

"Could be," she said. "He's known to be inappropriate with women colleagues."

"Find out and use it against him."

"I don't want to campaign that way."

"It works."

"Not for me," she said. "It damn sure don't. I'm running on my record."

"With Knox's money."

She tightened her lips and gripped the steering wheel hard, her shoulders hunched with tension. Mick figured he'd gone too far. He didn't mind, it was usually the other way around with her. This barely made a dent in all the times she'd admonished him.

Linda drove to Rocksalt and dropped him at her house.

"See you later," she said. "I'm going to visit Mrs. Combs's daughters."

Mick nodded and called Jacky, who said he'd gathered parts and would start work on the truck the following day. Mick ended the call and took a nap.

Chapter Eleven

The next morning Mick walked two miles, shifted to a jog for four miles, then ran hard up Lyons Avenue. His leg didn't bother him. His muscles and breath were returning. Linda was already gone, and he ate a breakfast of yogurt and fruit. Without the Percocet he dreamed more. The night before, he'd awakened with a gasp, covered in sweat, seeing the face of the enemy who'd triggered the IED.

He called Albin, and they drove to the cabin. Jacky had done a pretty fair job of clearing the road—the small brush and weeds were gone, and the saplings chopped down. There were occasional patches of yellow clay dirt, but he'd managed to leave enough ground cover to prevent the dirt from washing away at the first hard rain. The hood of the truck was raised, and Jacky leaned into the engine compartment, one foot precariously placed on an upended spackle bucket, his other leg gently bouncing in the air for balance. At the sound of the taxi, he slid backward to the earth. He held a wrench and wore light blue coveralls with a vertical pinstripe pattern smudged by grease.

"Oil filter," he said, "air filter, belts, spark plugs, distributor cap, radiator hoses. When I'm done, this rig'll run like a scalded dog."

"How long?"

"Three days ort to do it."

"What about the tires?" Mick said.

"Ain't got to them yet. Four new ones yonder."

He pointed to a stack of tires behind the truck.

"How are you paying for all this?" Mick said.

"Gave your name at the parts store and tire place."

"If you use a credit card, I can pay you back cash."

"Ain't got one," Jacky said. "Don't believe in them. Nobody's business what I spend my money on. I ain't winding up in some big government computer turned into a string of numbers."

Mick nodded and went in the house, which was as tidy as he'd left it before. Several cardboard boxes were stacked in the center of the front room. His grandfather's bed was in the disarray of having been slept in. An open suitcase contained a wad of clothing. He went back outside. Jacky's legs protruded from the engine compartment, the rest of his body inside. Satisfied that Jacky was making headway, Mick got in the taxi. Albin negotiated the road, more of a wide path, down the steep hill to the blacktop. His speed was uncharacteristically slow.

"Something bothering you?" Mick said.

"Yeah."

"About Jacky?"

"Naw. It's that dog bowl under the tree yesterday. I keep seeing it in my head. That old lady trying to feed a dog she didn't know was dead. It's the saddest thing I ever did see."

"She didn't strike me as being all that upset about Skippy."

"Me neither. I didn't know that dog. But I do know dog food, and it got me low."

Mick nodded and watched the land flow by. Stretching his arm out the window, he snatched a low-hanging seedpod from a maple. He'd called them "helicopters" as a kid due to their whirling flight. He squeezed out the seed and ate it. The inside of the seedpod was damp and he carefully affixed it to his nose. Albin noticed and began laughing.

"Where to, boss?" he said.

"College. I got to meet the geologist at three."

"We got some time. Want to eat lunch?"

An hour later they were finishing hamburgers and fries at a picnic table beside the Dairy Queen. They used rocks to anchor napkins against the sudden gusts. Hundreds of people had carved their names into the wooden surface, the older ones varnished over several times. A thirty-year record of customers that lay side by side like cuneiform. Albin triumphantly pointed out his name, dated six years before.

"There, by God," he said. "I set right here with Ida Gayheart. She ate a candy bar Blizzard and I had me a hot fudge sundae."

"Pretty good memory, there, Albin."

"I lived in Eldridge County all my life. Ain't that much to forget."

Mick nodded. His tendency was to recall things that made him sad—loss and sorrow, mistakes and missteps. He wondered if he simply lacked good memories or the capacity to focus on them later. As a kid he'd dearly wanted to eat at the Dairy Queen, but nobody took him. Now that he finally had, it was disappointing. He thought of his almost ex-wife and the child she was raising, and hoped she brought the little girl to the Dairy Queen in Owingsville. He shook his head twice to clear his mind.

Albin was still talking about Ida Gayheart, who she'd married, where she lived, and how many kids she had.

"Let's go up to the college," Mick said.

Dr. Harker was alone in her office. He took the guest chair, and she sat behind her desk, looking at him straight on. They exchanged minimal pleasantries.

"Did you have time to examine the dirt?" he said.

"Yes, and there's an anomaly," she said. "The analysis is simple. It's local clay dirt with a heavy component of limestone."

"Heavy?"

"Not weight. Heavy as in more than usual. Plenty of limestone around, but the ratio is very high in this sample. And the limestone is powdery."

"Like driveway dust?"

"Yes and no. Limestone for home use is what they call 'dense grade,' meaning it contains smaller gravel and dust. That helps it bond to the surface and hold up longer. Less likely to run off in a rain. This is more pure. The kind of powder you'd find at a quarry. The closest one is in Bourbon County, about an hour away. But dust from there would contain evidence of the machinery used to extract it. Oil. Fuel. Metal shavings."

She tilted back in her desk chair, lifting her eyebrows slightly. Mick understood she was waiting for him to ask a question. Dangling information was a basic method of interrogation, one he'd employed many times in Afghanistan and Iraq. It meant she had an agenda. He decided to comply.

"But it had something, right?" he said.

"No, nothing. That's what's odd. I asked a colleague to examine it, a chemistry guy. Where'd this dirt come from?"

"Dead guy's boots."

"What did he die of?"

"Bullets."

"What did he do?" she said. "Your dead guy."

"Sold heroin."

"All this effort for a drug dealer?"

"His job doesn't matter. I'd do the same for you."

"Is there a reward or something?"

"No, I'm working pro bono."

"Why?" she said.

"I don't have anything better to do."

She laughed abruptly, her face transforming into that of a child overcome by mirth. As her expression relaxed, he noticed small lines around her mouth and eyes, and understood she often laughed but maybe not in her office dealing with a stranger. She stood and offered her hand.

"I'll call you," she said, "when I hear from the chemistry prof."

"Thank you," he said, and left.

Outside he found Albin smoking a cigarette and leaning casually against a set of brick steps as if he'd posed himself for a photograph. He'd brushed his hair. The cab was parked half a block away. Mick understood that he'd distanced himself from his job to impress two college women who walked the opposite sidewalk. After they passed without noticing him, Albin crossed the street and took up a new post. Behind Mick came the sound of footsteps, and he moved out of the way for a young woman with a backpack, a cell phone in her hip pocket, and a ponytail strung through a special hole in the rear of her ball cap. She smiled at Mick. Albin threw his cigarette away and joined Mick.

"No luck?" Mick said.

"It's like they're blind to me. I don't know why. I'm okay looking, right? Do you think so?"

"You're a squared-away guy, Albin."

"Is it my hair?"

"No," Mick said. "It's your boots. Women look at a man's shoes."

"They're comfortable driving."

"Well, you ain't driving now, are you? You're out here complaining."

"I ain't complaining. I'm putting myself about. Can't help it if they don't know what they're missing out on. I got a job, and I live on my own."

Mick contemplated such simple advantages. In his own way, he had neither. His cell phone buzzed. The caller ID said "JB," and he answered.

"Hello, Johnny Boy."

"Linda said to call you. She's got a man dead, wants you there."

"Where?"

"Up Rodburn Holler. She said you'll see the cars."

Ten minutes later, Albin drove past a new grade school on the site of the old drive-in movie theater, which had been built on a former landfill. Albin turned left onto Rodburn Road, a single-lane blacktop with no ditch. One side of the holler lay in shadow half the day, then the other side. Only at noon did the road receive direct sun.

Chapter Twelve

Johnny Boy arrived first, saw the body, and immediately felt sick to his stomach. To avoid contaminating any evidence, he ran into the woods and threw up. At the creek he splashed water on his clothes, then stood in a patch of sun hoping the damp spots dried before anyone noticed.

Two city cops arrived next, then Linda. She didn't mention his wet clothing but focused on the body. It lay facedown in a strip of wild clover. The back of the man's shirt was stained with dried blood.

"Any idea who it is?" she said.

"Could be anybody. Dressed like all of us. Jeans, boots, work shirt."

"I can see that, Johnny Boy."

"I'm observing the crime scene, Sheriff."

"Anything else you observed?"

He pointed to a two-door sedan.

"That car yonder."

"Know it?" she said.

"Nope. It's a Ford. Half the county drives one. Could be somebody picnicking. Or kids up a trail smoking weed."

A city policeman joined them, an older man with a polished name tag on his black shirt that read "Sgt. Blevins." Johnny Boy had known him and his wife for many years.

"Hey, Faron," he said.

Faron dropped his chin in greeting.

"How's Brandi?" Johnny Boy said.

"Doing good. Started herself a little online business selling birdhouses. All kinds of shapes. Plus custom jobs."

"A custom birdhouse?"

"People want a model of their own homes mostly. Or their church. They send a photograph in email. Brandi builds it and paints it to match."

"Any money in it?"

"Not yet," Faron said. "Not enough, anyhow, but it keeps her busy, and she likes it. You doing all right, Linda?"

"Wore out from putting up signs," she said.

"I see them all over the place."

"Who you reckon that is laying there?" she said.

"Don't know yet," Faron said. "We're waiting on Marquis to get here. Can't touch the body till he pronounces him. He's dead though. I checked his neck vein. Nothing."

"What about that car?"

"No plates or registration," Faron said. "Might be an off-the-gridder."

"Or somebody wants to slow us down," Linda said.

They regarded the body silently. Despite the small talk there was a palpable sense of frustration, like a horse chewing at the bit and ready to run. They couldn't begin their work until Marquis did his, which depended on his duties at the funeral home. Embalming wasn't a task that could bear much in the way of a delay. It couldn't be rushed either. If there was a memorial service, hours might pass before he arrived.

A car engine whined in low gear, and they turned to see Assistant Chief Chet Logan from the Rocksalt Police Department slowly disembark. He was a big man who'd been shot in the line of duty and moved slowly. Everybody liked him, even the people he took into custody. He was on track to be chief in a couple of years.

"Faron," he said. "You ranking officer?"

"Yes, sir."

"We got a little problem," Chet said. "Linda, you need to hear this, too. Chief wants us to double-check jurisdiction. The city limits runs right along here. We ain't for sure if the body is in town or the county."

"It's either yours or mine," Linda said. "Is that what you're saying?"

"About the size of it. Chief's sending a surveyor over with a plat. The boundary line got mixed up when they developed all this."

Another car drove along the road, and everyone turned to the sound, assuming it was Marquis or the surveyor. Instead it was a taxi.

"Albin, ain't it?" said Faron. "Who's that with him?"

"My brother," Linda said.

"Ain't seen him in fifteen years," Chet said.

They watched Mick walk their way, his boots moving over the grass with no sound. Shorter than everyone, including Linda, he exuded a sense of restrained power. He nodded to the group.

"Hidy, Mick," said Chet. "What do you know? All on your own self and afraid to tell it?"

Mick nodded, his face twitching in what passed for a slight grin.

"Hey, Chet," he said. "How you getting along?"

"Better before all this. We don't know who it is, and we can't touch him. What are you doing here?"

"I asked him to consult," Linda said. "He works homicides in the army. That is, if the body's in the county."

Johnny Boy looked at the sky. A buzzard was circling on a thermal. It had made it to the body quicker than the medical examiner.

"I know that red Taurus," Mick said. "It's Mason Kissick's. I was in it the other day. My bet, that's your body. About five seven with light hair. Scar on the back of his left hand in an L shape."

"You remember all that?" Faron said.

"Yeah. I remember too much mostly."

Chet jerked his chin to Faron. Faron approached the body at an angle, stepping carefully to avoid any bent grass that could be evidence. The left arm was splayed out, palm down.

"Yep," Faron said. "L shape like it got laid open on glass."

The county surveyor arrived with large scrolls under his arm, followed by Marquis in his cheap suit, carrying a portable medical bag made of leather. Johnny Boy turned away immediately. Marquis was a nice enough guy, always willing to contribute to community events, but ghosts scared Johnny Boy, and he was convinced that Marquis trafficked among them professionally.

Marquis moved to the body, pronounced the man dead, and waited for assistance. Mick helped roll the body onto its back. He'd been shot in the throat and the chest. Grisly business done, Marquis began walking away, staying in the bright sun from the west.

"It's Mason Kissick," Mick said. "I know the family."

"We all know the damn family," Chet said.

"I can do the notification," Mick said.

"Wouldn't be official," Chet said.

"You're right," Linda said. "How about I deputize my brother long enough for him to go talk to Shifty? That's her second boy dead in a week. Mick's friendly with her."

Chet shrugged and waited for Mick.

"Could be a conflict of interest," Mick said.

"What kind of conflict?" Faron said.

"I have authority over military but not civilians."

"You're the only soldier around," Faron said. "It's not like you're going to arrest yourself."

"Linda already took care of that," Chet said.

He laughed, and everyone joined, including Mick.

"I don't want to go out there," Johnny Boy said. "Mason was a buddy of mine from high school."

"All right," Linda said. "Mick is temporarily deputized to give the death notice but not make arrests."

A long group silence indicated consent, and Albin drove Mick to the Kissicks'. Mick looked out the car window, thinking about spring in general—the hills soaring with new life, unseen energy pushing buds toward the sun. The season had a melancholy undercurrent. Each year the land refreshed itself while humanity aged. The beauty of nature concealed its inherent brutality, but people laid themselves bare.

Albin parked in the yard. Mick left the car and slowly walked the pale grass flecked with violets and dandelions. He stomped the porch to let Mrs. Kissick know she had a visitor, then knocked on the door, waited a minute, and knocked harder. Maybe she was around back or in the bathroom. He knocked a third time.

"Mrs. Kissick," he yelled. "It's Mick Hardin. Can I come in a minute?"

He heard a woman's voice but no words, which he interpreted as a welcome. He opened the door. Mrs. Kissick sat in her corner chair, the little revolver on an end table beside a coffee cup. She held a .410 shotgun aimed at Mick's belly. The barrel had been sawn down to the size of an old-time flintlock pistol but more lethal. In her other hand was a phone.

"Is it him?" she said.

"Yes, ma'am. Mason's dead."

People thought a growth spurt was the exclusive province of childhood, but he watched her become suddenly older, the years amassing themselves on the skin of her face. It was awful to witness. She waved the shotgun barrel for him to sit on the couch. He moved with great care, and she laid the weapon across her thighs.

"Graveyard dirt ain't even tamped down yet," she said, "and I got to dig another hole."

"Do you need anything?"

"I need my kids back."

"Anybody you want me to call? Somebody to stay with you."

"I called my daughter and son. My last boy."

Her gray face softened, and he thought she was going to weep, but her expression hardened itself like clay in a kiln. He glanced away to avoid drawing her rage.

"What's his name?" he said gently. "The boy you called."

"Raymond. We call him Ray-Ray."

"Where's he live?"

"San Diego."

"Long ways away," he said.

"He's coming in tomorrow."

Mick nodded. She hadn't moved since he sat but watched a distant area known only to her, what the old vets called a "thousand-yard stare." Blank and seemingly

unfocused. She could be seeing Mason and Barney as chil-
dren, or nothing at all.

"Mrs. Kissick," he said. "Can I get you some coffee?"

She didn't answer, and he went to the kitchen. The
appliances were new, contrasting with the worn linoleum,
scuffed bare before the sink and stove. He poured two cups
of coffee and carried them to the living room. She was
immobile as a statue. He moved into her view, circling
wider than necessary, and placed her coffee beside the cell
phone.

"Here you go," he said.

She nodded her thanks and sipped the coffee. Her eyes
refocused on him.

"If you ain't caring," he said, "I'd like to ask you a few
questions. Might help me figure out who did it."

"Killed Mason, you mean?"

"Yes, ma'am."

"All right."

"We found his car," Mick said. "Do you know where
he was?"

"Up Rodburn Holler."

"Yes, ma'am. I mean before that. Where'd he go?"

She held the coffee cup against her forehead to warm
her face. Mick could hear a clock ticking, the refrigerator's
hum. She drank more coffee. Her head sank toward her
chest, and she closed her eyes. A line of tears ran down her
face. She ignored it and spoke in a whisper.

"I sent him out," she said.

"Where to?"

"To get Barney's stash."

She inhaled deeply and drank more coffee.

"We're in a peck of trouble," she said.

"Maybe I can help."

"Nobody can."

"Talk to me."

She lifted the cup to her mouth and drank like a bird, then gulped the last of it. Her body straightened, and she looked at the shotgun as if she'd forgotten it was there. She leaned it against the wall and set the coffee cup on the table.

"Barney got his dope from Detroit," she said. "Charley Flowers sent it down once a month. Barney paid at delivery. They worked it that way for a couple of years. Barney was smart. He . . ."

Her voice trailed away, imbued with sorrow.

"He what, Mrs. Kissick? Did something happen?"

"Him and Charley Flowers made a deal."

"A new one?"

"Barney had something lined up, a onetime thing, a big sale. Said it was his last deal, then he was getting out. He paid half up front and was going to pay off the rest after he sold it."

"Do you know who he was selling it to?"

"No, he never said."

"Did the deal fall through or something?"

"No, the problem was he didn't know where to keep that much stuff. Used to, he'd spread it around here and there, them little packets. But he wanted it all in one place for the big sale. Not here or in a car or shed or anything."

"What's the trouble you're in?"

"Charley Flowers wants the rest of his money. He called me."

"He had your number?"

"Yes. I talked to him sometimes. If Barney couldn't get reception, I passed messages between them."

"How much money?"

"Two hundred thousand."

"Did you tell him Barney was dead?"

"He didn't care. 'A debt's a debt,' he said. I don't have that kind of money."

Mick nodded, turning things over in his mind. He didn't think Charley Flowers was behind the murders—it made no sense to kill a distributor before getting the money. It was possible that somebody else knew about the heroin. Maybe they killed Mason and took it. Or maybe they were still looking for it.

"Mrs. Kissick," he said. "Did Mason know where the heroin was?"

She nodded, staring out the window. Clouds obscured the sky above the tree line, turning the air a flat gray. Mick was losing her.

"Did Barney tell him where it was?" he said.

"No, I did."

She was quiet for nearly a minute. Mick understood that she wanted to speak, was gearing up to say something important. He'd seen the same hesitation during interrogations in the desert. It required patience and delicacy on his part, combined with timing. He squatted on the floor before her, making sure his head was below hers, then looked up at her.

"How did you know where Barney hid the heroin?"

Her voice was a raspy whisper.

"I told him where," she said. "The old Mushroom Mines. He put it in there maybe a month back. It's in a blue suitcase, belonged to my aunt."

"Why there?"

"It's big. Everybody's scared to go in there."

He watched her mind slip away from the conversation, staring into a middle distance, perhaps recalling happier times before she lost her sons. Now was the time for Mick to push harder, take advantage of her vulnerability to gain further information. Instead, he opened her phone and asked which number belonged to Charley Flowers. She pointed to a 313 area code. He input the digits into his phone and looked at her again, a gray-headed lady with two small weapons and no protectors.

Chapter Thirteen

The old Stepside sat in the yard with the hood up and the windows rolled down. Jacky Turner revved the engine, listening for any odd sounds that might require further adjustment. Twice he'd driven it off the hill to the blacktop and back to the cabin, then tightened the suspension. Satisfied, he cut the engine and returned to his paramount project: self-repairing car doors made of nitinol.

He'd gotten the idea from a brand of special paper clips that could be bent and twisted but would return to their original shape when dropped into hot water. Jacky reasoned that driving a damaged automobile through a heated car wash would smooth the dents. In a pinch you could use a hair dryer. The problem was acquiring a sufficient amount of nitinol for experimentation.

Three secondary projects were still in the preliminary stages of sketches and notes—a device to prevent Pringles from breaking, a method to easily open the stiff plastic sheaths that enclosed new batteries, and a method to protect light bulbs better than lightly padded cardboard open at both ends. He heard a car climbing the hill. A taxi crested the rise and stopped at the wide spot where the yard merged with woods. Jacky underwent a wild surge of hope that it contained a representative from the patent office. Instead it was the property owner, who left the car and crossed the yard.

"Hey, Jacky," Mick said. "How's the truck?"

"Runs like a sewing machine. Needs gas."

"You warm enough at night?"

"Yeah. I made a little fire in the stove. Couple of chunks, and I'm good. Found an ax in the shed. You know an ax is a simple machine, right? There's six of them, but I've been thinking on a seventh."

"A spring?" Mick said. "Like that Slinky escalator?"

"No, a spring doesn't change force. What I'm onto is something else. Still in the research stage, if you know what I mean."

"Classified?"

Jacky nodded, grateful for Mick's understanding of the security necessary to his development phase.

"You're getting some work done, then," Mick said.

"Nice and quiet. No distractions. You got a blacksnake living under the porch, but we get along all right."

"That's Roscoe," Mick said. "He's been the house snake for ten years. Before that, probably his mom or dad. I used to feed Roscoe baby bats."

They stared at the porch for a couple of minutes, each thinking about Roscoe under there, resting, digesting, or preparing to hunt. The only drawback to blacksnakes was their occasional decision to hibernate with copperheads. They couldn't mate, but they snuggled through the long months of winter. Their dual appearance in spring could be disconcerting.

Mick arranged for Jacky to stay at the cabin another week for security. He paid Albin, gave him a bonus, and sent him on his way. After taking one last look at the cabin he loved, Mick got in the pickup and drove off the hill. He made a few quick turns to test the steering, then checked the brakes and acceleration. The old truck ran better than it had in years. At the blacktop he had sufficient cell service to call his sister, who was still waiting for the surveyor's decision. She knew little about the Mushroom Mines but suggested he talk to Johnny Boy, who'd grown up near them.

Mick drove to the sheriff's office. The new dispatcher, Sandra Caldwell, introduced herself.

"Didn't we meet?" Mick said.

"Not really. I saw you in here a few days ago. Linda said she made you a deputy. Need a badge?"

"No, thank you. It's temporary. Might be over already."

"That was quick," she said.

She smiled, the tip of her tongue visible below her slight overbite. Her ears were small and unadorned, her dark hair pulled into a yellow barrette fortified by a couple of bobby pins.

"Your bobby pins," he said. "They're upside down."

"What?"

"The flat side is supposed to be faceup. That way the little ridges hold on to your scalp. They won't slide out."

"How do you know something like that?"

"Something I picked up along the way," he said. "I remembered it when I noticed yours."

"Thank you," she said. "It's nice to be noticed."

Mick nodded.

"Anything else?" she said.

"Need to see Johnny Boy."

"I meant that you noticed about me?"

She looked at him with a warm expression that made him uncomfortable. He studied her in case he'd missed something but didn't know what she meant. She tilted her head, smiling. He turned away quickly and entered the deputy's office, a small room made smaller by banks of file cabinets on all four walls. Johnny Boy glared as Mick sat uninvited in the guest chair.

"Your cousin got the truck running," Mick said.

"He can fix anything. How's the Kissicks?"

"No damn good. Her boy's coming in."

"Raymond. About your age. Joined the service and ain't been seen since. Some folks thought he got killed in Afghanistan, but he didn't."

"It's that memory I need, Johnny Boy."

"About the Kissicks? You know as much as I do."

"No, about the Mushroom Mines."

"First time I went in I was eight years old. Had a flashlight and some string wrapped around a stick like kids on TV. I didn't get very far. The light was too weak and the string was too short. A few years later I started going back. Supposed to be a big pond in there, and I thought maybe albino fish would be in it. Read about them in a book."

"Was there?"

"Not a one."

"What'd they mine in there? Clay?"

"No, it was never a mine. It was a limestone quarry. There's a lot of tunnels and big rooms. I mean huge. They hauled rock out with mules. It ran twenty-four hours a day, seven days a week. On Sunday they had church in there. Pretty interesting history if you're interested."

Mick nodded.

"After World War II it set empty for twenty-some years. Then a bunch of farmers teamed up with hippies and started growing mushrooms in it."

"Hippies?" Mick said. "Around here?"

"They came down in the sixties. First with VISTA, you know, the War on Poverty and all that. A bunch of them stuck around. They had a commune. Hippie Holler, everybody called it. Went around half naked half the time."

"They grew mushrooms?" Mick said. "Psilocybin?"

"No, the regular kind. Somebody was pretty smart behind it. They got state money to level out the floors and put in ventilation. Dark as heck, real humid, and never got too cold or too hot. It was ideal for mushrooms. Cheap, too. A low overhead, so to speak."

Mick nodded to acknowledge Johnny Boy's attempt at making humor.

"But here's the best part," Johnny Boy said. "The big horse farms in Lexington clear out their stalls twice a day. They paid the mushroom people to haul it off. Couple of times a week they drove a load to the old quarry and filled a few rooms. They started in growing mushrooms to sell. Like I said, smart. They rented the quarry for nothing and got paid for the manure to grow it in. And they'd never run out of space. Place made a lot of money for about four years. Then it shut down. Never gave out no reason, but a lot of talk."

"What kind of talk?"

"The bad kind," Johnny Boy said. "Real bad."

A chair scraped the floor in the foyer. Sandra knocked on the office door and stepped into view.

"I have to go," she said. "Got to drop off some cholesterol pills with my aunt."

"Right," Johnny Boy said. "I'll hold the fort."

"Did I hear y'all talking about the Mushroom Mines? My great-uncle worked there."

"Is he still alive?" Mick said.

"Oh yeah. He's tougher than a night in jail."

"I'd like to talk to him if that's all right."

"Maybe later," she said. "I can't be late."

She left. Johnny Boy watched her, then became self-conscious and glanced at Mick.

"She's a good worker," Johnny Boy said. "Good to her family."

Mick nodded. Those were the highest compliments in the hills, which meant Johnny Boy liked her more than he was willing to let on.

"The quarry," Mick said. "Anything else?"

Johnny Boy opened one of the gunmetal-gray filing cabinets and withdrew a folder, frayed at the edges and discolored. It was surprisingly thick. He set the first several pages aside and studied the rest.

"About sixteen years ago some big outfit from California bought it. They figured it was a good setup for data storage. One road in and out. Chambers were already there. The tunnels are big enough for cars to drive around. Ceilings are twenty-six feet high. They named it the Stone Mountain Ultra-Secure Dataplex. Nobody around here called it that."

Johnny Boy flicked through the pages then read aloud.

"Let's see here. It says 'four hundred thousand square feet of subterranean data storage. A carrier-neutral facility.' I don't know what that is."

"It means independent of any one network provider. More flexible and cheaper. No downtime."

Johnny Boy gave him a quizzical look.

"The army has them," Mick said. "They call it a 'carrier hotel.'"

Johnny Boy thumbed through the file.

"Construction began in '08. The company had an office on Tom T. Hall Boulevard in Olive Hill. They blocked up all the quarry entrances except the main one, then started building outside."

He took a deep breath and stared out the window. His voice took a wistful tone.

"I was in school then. This dataplex was going to save the county. Supposed to hire fifteen hundred people when it was done. About seven construction companies worked on it—cement, electrical, concrete block, framing. Then a big problem. Nobody got paid. It was some kind of scam. The whole thing stopped in 2009."

"Why do you have a file on it?" Mick said. "It's state and federal, not county."

"Back before all this, in 2004, there was a county matter. Two bodies were found in there, a married couple. Turns out the man's son and his girlfriend killed them. They're still in prison. That was on file, and I added the dataplex info to it."

"Anything else I ort to know about?"

"A lot of rumor and gossip. Haunted by ghosts. Satanists doing stuff in there. Mainly it was a place kids went to smoke weed and drink beer. Then they'd scare each other."

"What's its current status?"

"Been on the market for twelve years. They're calling it Mega Mountain now. A few months ago I heard it got bought but didn't pay no attention. Anything old gets a lot of stories put to it."

Mick nodded. The same was true for covered bridges, empty houses, and elderly people living alone. It would happen with Mrs. Kissick next. The sheriff's office phone rang. Johnny Boy answered, wrote information on a pad, and hung up. He stood and put on his hat.

"You're a deputy now," he said. "Best stay here and man the phones. I got to go."

"What's the call?"

"Problem at the Dollar General."

Johnny Boy left fast, and Mick was suddenly alone in the three-room suite of offices with no task at hand. The filing cabinets were surprisingly well organized. He found a section marked *C* easily and looked for Sandra's last name. No Caldwells had been arrested. He went to the foyer and peeked through the door glass at the empty parking lot, then searched her desk and found the standard supplies of official forms, letterhead, and envelopes. Personal items were in the bottom drawer: sugarless gum, hand lotion, hairbrush, pocketknife, and a phone charger.

Tucked into the kneehole were a pair of tennis shoes and a collapsible umbrella. The right side of the desk had a telephone with a shoulder rest attached to the receiver. In one corner stood a small framed photograph of a man and woman in the slightly faded colors of old Kodak. Mick concluded that Sandra was right-handed, close to her family, and prepared for contingencies. That described most of the people in the county. He chuckled to himself. With such ace detective skills, no wonder he was a lowly deputy.

He heard a car engine and quickly stepped to the front of the foyer, seeing his sister park and disembark from the big SUV. Linda strode across the lot in a brisk fashion, her face etched with tension.

"I'm off the hook," she said. "The body's in the city by four feet. Thank you, Jesus. Get anything from Mason's mom?"

"She's pretty tore up. Johnny Boy's on a call."

"What are you doing here, anyway?"

"You deputized me," he said. "I'm here being a deputy."

"Snooping, if I know you."

"A little, yeah. I'm waiting on the dispatcher. Need to talk to her great-uncle."

"That old man's a suspect?"

"No," Mick said. "He used to work at the Mushroom Mines."

Linda lifted both hands palms-out in a gesture of halt. She shook her head so hard her ponytail slapped the side of her head. Mick recognized the response from when they were kids and he showed her something from the woods that offended her town sensibilities—a dead frog, a nightcrawler tied in a knot around his finger, a wriggling salamander held between his lips.

"I don't have time for this," she said. "I've got paper-work, then court."

"Big case?"

"They're all big cases to someone."

"Let me guess. Two dogs in a tree."

"Not funny, Big Bro. I got four campaign events today—Kiwanis Club breakfast. A fish fry at the VFW. Some kind of speech at the Lions Club. Then a spaghetti supper with the Rotary. If I win, I'll have to get a bigger uniform from all the eating."

Linda's cell phone rang. She answered, listened, and ended the call.

"That was Johnny Boy," she said. "He's got a hostage situation at the Dollar General."

They hurried to the car and sped two miles with the light bar flashing. A crowd of people stood in the parking lot. Linda parked beside the front, where the manager was helping an older woman with a cane.

"Anyone else inside?" Linda said.

"Mrs. Patton here is the last customer," the manager said. "Johnny Boy's in there."

"Don't let anyone in the building."

Linda entered, with Mick following. Johnny Boy's voice echoed oddly from the rear, and Linda headed straight for him. Mick went left in a flanking maneuver that took him to the back wall. Midway down the long lane he saw Linda and Johnny Boy talking in front of a closed door. He joined them.

"It's Jaybird Watts," Johnny Boy said. "He works here. Says he's got somebody hostage."

"What's he want?" Linda said.

"Eight hundred forty dollars or he'll start shooting."

"Tell him we're getting the money together," Linda said. "I'll talk to the manager. Keep him talking, Johnny Boy. I'll find out who he's got in there."

Johnny Boy nodded and turned back to the door. Linda went outside while Mick retrieved a yellow plastic bag from behind the checkout counter. In the paper aisle he opened four packages of napkins and dumped them in the bag. He returned to the front and opened the cash register. He spread all the one-dollar bills over the napkins, then added fives, tens, and a few twenties on top.

Linda entered the store holding a set of keys on a ring with a Bigfoot fob.

"It was shift change," she said. "Eight employees, plus the manager. Two unaccounted for. There's a back door for cargo. I got a key."

"All right," Mick said. "If you get your car, I'll meet you at the loading dock. Can I have that key?"

She tossed him Bigfoot, then went to confer with Johnny Boy. Mick left the building and walked through the crowd of evacuated shoppers. He passed a two-door ice freezer and a locked metal cabinet for propane tank exchange. The rear had a narrow alley with a garage door made of corrugated stainless steel. It was partially open, exposing the bottom three feet of interior space.

Mick squatted and closed his eyes briefly to allow his pupils to contract, then peered in. Cardboard boxes of detergent were stacked on the left. The other side had a row of shelving filled with dry goods. A light in the rear illuminated a man sitting in a plastic chair holding a pint of cheap whiskey. He wore a feed-store cap high on his head, and a stubby ponytail in a tight band hung over his collar. A cell phone in a bowl was playing a tinny version of "Free Bird." He appeared to be unarmed. Mick ducked under the door and stepped inside.

"Hey, man," he said.

"Holy shit," Jaybird said. "Where'd you up from?"

"I got your money. You got a gun or anything?"

"At the house. But not on me, no."

"Anybody else in here?"

"Naw, just me and Skynyrd. Johnny Boy's on the other side of the door."

"Where's the hostage?"

"I just said that to get the money."

Mick nodded. The man sipped his whiskey. The nearest weapon was a mop, but Jaybird would have to stand and pull it out of a large bucket on wheels.

"What's all this about?" Mick said.

"A necklace. My girlfriend showed it to me online. She wants it bad. And I want her bad. You know how it goes."

"Buddy, I do," Mick said. "Would they not let you buy it on time?"

"She didn't want to wait. She'd got it all picked out in her mind. Said she saw it up there at some big mall at Lexington Green."

Jaybird stretched his arm to rap on the door.

"Hey, Johnny Boy," he said. "You still there?"

"Right here," came the muffled voice.

"What's the name of that big mall they got at Lexington Green?"

"The Mall at Lexington Green."

"Yeah, what's its name?"

"The Mall at Lexington Green."

"Yes, doggone it. Can you not hear me through this door?"

"I hear good, Jaybird. The mall up there is called the Mall at Lexington Green."

"You're shitting me."

"Nope," Johnny Boy said.

"That's the dumbest name I ever did hear for a mall."

"Reckon they thought it would be easy to remember."

Jaybird shook his head and took a long drink of whiskey.

"You think he'll arrest me?" he said.

"Maybe," Mick said. "I don't know that you broke any laws. Nothing says a man can't lock himself in and get drunk. I've done it many a time."

Jaybird offered the bottle.

"You want some?" he said.

"Can't right now. Just got off pills for a hurt leg. I'd hate to get drunk and fall. Then you'd have to help me out of here."

"I'd do it, bub. Damn sure would. Reckon I'll get fired over this?"

"Well," Mick said, "I ain't a manager, but I'd say you might get suspended or something. Depends on all kinds of things."

"Like what?"

"How long you been with the company. If you missed a bunch of work. What your main job is. Probably comes down to if the boss man likes you. Most things do."

Jaybird stuck out his bottom lip as he considered Mick's words. He took a quick drink of whiskey.

"You got eight forty in that bag?" Jaybird said.

"No, about a hundred. It's mostly napkins."

"What brand?"

"Smart and Simple, I believe it was."

"A dollar for a hundred and fifty napkins. That's half a cent apiece. I don't see how they make any money on them."

"It's more like two-thirds of a cent apiece."

"There's the profit, then."

Mick nodded. Jaybird reached in his pocket as if for a cigarette, then looked at his hand, disappointed.

"You got a cigarette?" Jaybird said.

"Don't smoke. Y'all sell them?"

"Yeah, the main brands. None of that fancy organic stuff."

CHRIS OFFUTT

"There's probably a bunch back here somewhere."

"Naw, that'd be stealing," Jaybird said. "Whatever I am, I ain't never been a thief."

"You about ready to leave?"

"Oh, yeah. Waiting on you."

Jaybird finished the bottle and gathered his cell phone from the bowl. He tapped on the door.

"Johnny Boy," he said.

"Right here, man."

"I'll talk to you later. Tell your mom and them I said hidy."

Mick took the bottle, and they headed for the garage door. A long chain dangled in a loop, and Jaybird pulled it to raise the door. Linda stood in a wide stance, holster unsnapped. Jaybird stiffened, and Mick gripped his upper arm tightly.

"You law?" Jaybird said to him.

"No. She's my sister."

"Where's the hostage?" Linda said.

"I believe Jaybird took himself hostage," Mick said.

"What?" Linda said.

"Just him. No weapon. If everybody sees you out front, it'll be good for the election. Let him go tomorrow, and you'll get his family votes, too."

"You should be my campaign manager."

"Are you looking for one?" Jaybird said. "I'm probably out of a job for a spell."

Linda called Johnny Boy and told him to meet them at the police vehicle. She studied Jaybird, then faced her brother.

"There's paperwork, Deputy."

"Can't do it, Sis. I have to put this money back in the cash register. Then I got to go see your dispatcher's great-uncle."

"Johnny Boy won't like that. He's got a crush on her."

"Make him out the hero of Dollar General. It'll all work out."

Mick faced Jaybird.

"Don't do nothing like this again," Mick said. "We might not be so friendly next time."

"What'll I tell my girlfriend?"

"The truth. You did it for her. She'll appreciate that. It's what they call a grand romantic gesture. You did your best."

"Yeah," Linda said. "You're a regular Romeo, Jaybird. Now give me your hands, I got to cuff you."

Mick returned the money to the cash register, opened his wallet, and placed four dollars on the counter to pay for the napkins. Outside he watched Linda escort her prisoner to the car, where Johnny Boy gently helped him in. Linda turned to the crowd and made a brief statement, while several people took photographs with their cell phones. Mick left, wondering how the napkin manufacturers made money on their products.

Chapter Fourteen

Brace Gifford was a man of action, even if that action consisted of sitting on his porch watching a robin's nest in a maple. The eggs hatched in the order they were laid, and the babies always departed the nest in the same sequence. On the ground below stood a tiny fledgling with tufts of down on its head. It was the first one to leave the nest, watched over by a nearby adult male. Brace wanted to see the next one jump from the nest, a move he considered the most courageous in nature—a bird too young to fly but willing to navigate the air. It invariably fell to the earth and lay stunned, then looked about and walked in an awkward circle.

Brace had never married and had lived the past sixty years of his life in the same house. He'd planted the maple that held the robin's nest and carefully cultivated three hackberry trees to feed the birds. A row of cedars bordered the north edge of his property, the trees serving as a windbreak in winter and giving the robins protective cover from predators. He watched the mother tear off bits of worm and feed her young, perhaps the last meal before one leaped into space.

A breeze carried the scent of automobile exhaust, and a few seconds later he heard an engine. He had no near neighbors. The mail had already run, bringing its standard fare of advertising circulars, which he saved year-round for winter kindling. Probably kids, he thought, out roaming the roads, seeking what little adventure there was to have. The car sound came closer, then stopped, and he heard a door open. Still gazing at the nest, he gestured for the vehicle's occupant to avoid the area in front of the tree. No sense in scaring the fledgling.

He saw his niece and a stranger, a shortish man, thin and wiry, slightly favoring one leg and trying not to show it. The man lacked a hat, which was unusual.

"Hey, Little Sandy," Brace said.

"Good to see you, Uncle Robin," Sandra said.

"Watch where you walk. Got a little feller there don't know how to fly yet."

"Reckon he'll make it?"

"Oh yeah. If a snake or a fox or a hawk don't get him."

"This is my uncle Brace," Sandra said. "I call him Uncle Robin on account of the birds."

"I'm Jimmy Hardin's boy," Mick said.

"Jimmy Hardin," Brace said. "Homer Jack's boy?"

"Yeah, Homer Jack was my grandfather."

"I knowed him. A good man. He could read the woods like a magazine. You'uns come up on the porch. I'd invite you in, but I got to keep an eye on that baby yonder."

He pointed to the fledgling, which was turning itself in a circle, one tiny wing aimed up like a spindle.

"Is it hurt, Uncle Robin?" Sandra said.

"Naw. It's getting the lay of the land. In a week, it'll be flying."

"Working its strength up," Mick said.

"That's right," Brace said. "If you look sharp, you'll see its daddy in that bush. He's learning the little feller how to get around for food."

Mick followed Sandra onto the porch. She sat on a low swing at the end, the rusty chain creaking from her weight. Brace eased beside her, and she leaned against him in a way Mick understood she'd done all her life. Brace patted her on the shoulder.

"What are you needing, Little Sandy?"

"Not a thing, Uncle Robin."

"That's good. How's that man of yours? I forget his name."

"So did I."

"Uh-huh," Brace said. "That's how it is now?"

"Yeah. I told you all about it."

"Well, I forgot that, too. You know how it goes. I'm getting up there."

"Are you eating and drinking water?"

"Oh yeah," Brace said. "When I remember."

He began laughing, a high-pitched giggle that ended in a series of snorts as if he were impersonating a hog. Sandra joined him, and Mick was surprised to hear the same puffing sounds issue from her mouth. He wondered if it was a family trait. The action of their laughter set the swing moving, and they rocked and snorted until the back of the swing struck the porch railing.

"Oh shit, oh dear," Sandra said. "We're about to go overboard!"

Brace stiffened his legs and halted the swing's motion. The excess chain dangling from a hook in the ceiling rattled against itself.

"What's the story, morning glory?" Brace said.

"Mick wants to talk to you, Uncle Robin."

Brace looked at the stranger, prepared to wait all day for him to speak. The man had pale blue eyes that shifted hue depending on the light. Brace thought he probably had two modes—full throttle or long pondering.

"Your niece," Mick said, "grand-niece, I reckon. She said you used to work at the old Mushroom Mines."

Brace tipped his chin an eighth inch in what passed for a nod.

"Long time ago," he said. "I was a pup."

"I'd like to hear about it, if you don't mind. The way the operation worked and all."

Brace had worked in the old quarry fifty years ago but still thought about it every few days. He'd expected the sheriff to arrive decades ago, then concluded that it was over and he was safe. Now, damned if Little Sandy hadn't brought a somebody sniffing around who had lawman written all over him.

"What's your interest?" Brace said.

"Near as I can figure, one of the Kissick boys hid something in the quarry. There's some trouble over it. Their mother asked me to help."

"Shifty Kissick?"

"Yeah, you might know her. Way she tells it, my daddy used to court her in the old days."

"Well, sir," Brace said. "Way I tell it, plenty of young fellers used to court her. Then that damned Darvis Kissick came along and run them everyone off. Your daddy, too. Her and Darvis had a bunch of kids."

"Five. Three boys are dead. I believe two of them got killed over something to do with the Mushroom Mines. What I'd appreciate is if you could tell me what you remember about the layout back then."

"The layout?"

"I heard they had a store in there."

"Yeah, buddy. Right inside the entrance. They had electric lights for a little office with a desk and a couple of chairs. Sold a carton of mushrooms for a dollar. Kept the money setting out in a cigar box. The mushrooms were the little white kind, size of a hickory nut. Folks drove up there and bought them. They cost more at the grocery store in town."

"Who was the boss of it?"

"They was three. One tiny little woman ran the store. I mean she was short. Everybody said if she got a job in the sun, she'd grow some. The other boss was a man with an accent from off. Not American, I don't think. You could tell by the way he walked and stood. People said he grew up on different dirt."

"I know what you mean," Mick said.

"Another man, he was the trucking boss. Twice a week, mushrooms got delivered to the grocery stores in Rocksalt and Grayson and a couple of gas stations. One truck had a run to Ashland. Stopped at Catlettsburg and Kenova. It was a loop. Up Sixty to Ashland, down Twenty-Three, then back."

"Pretty good memory."

"I was a driver. Got promoted out of the pickers."

"Must have been a good picker."

Brace became silent as if looking into the past on a screen inside his head. He remembered everything in a sudden burst, could see himself moving through the events as they unfolded. Still staring into an internal middle distance, he began talking. He'd just turned sixteen and wanted money for a car. Jobs were scarce, and he'd heard the quarry was hiring. He got a ride there in the morning, and a man named Warren Rockland gave him six large sacks and said to fill them before taking a break. Rockland had repeated himself four times, talking louder with each repetition. He told Brace to walk into the cave and keep going until he saw other people, then start picking. "No fights," he said. "No trouble. You take somebody else's bag and you're fired." He repeated this four times, too.

The chilly interior was lit by a series of bare bulbs from a wire hung on nails driven into beams. Each bulb illuminated a small area directly below, with most of the light either absorbed by the dark walls or dissipating into the sunless air. Brace could hear the rhythmic hum of a generator. The thick air was cool and smelled bad. The farther in he walked, the worse the smell became. The string of lights turned a corner into a massive chamber piled with horse manure in crude bins, the source of the overwhelming stench. He pulled his T-shirt over his nose and mouth. He sensed movement and spun on his heels, alarmed. In front of him stood a very tall man holding three full bags, a big smile on his face.

"Hidy," the man said, his loud voice echoing. "Pick mushroom."

He showed Brace the contents of his fullest sack, a mound of white mushrooms specked with manure like dirty gravel.

"Pick mushroom," the man said again. "You pick mushroom."

He turned away and within a few seconds was invisible in the darkness. Brace squinted after him, listening to his footsteps fade. An hour later he'd filled one bag and encountered two more pickers, a man and a woman, both older than him, both barely able to communicate. Brace wondered if it was a reaction to breathing the foul air.

Despite the damp cold, he was sweating from exertion—the constant moving, bending over, and digging through manure for the tiny white baubles. Sweat gathered in his eyebrows and trickled into his eyes. He couldn't wipe it away because manure covered his hands. He moved into another room, one of many that interlocked through passageways. Alone in the dark, covered in animal shit, Brace became disoriented and anxious. He decided to quit, unable to understand how the other workers could tolerate such conditions. He followed the lights to another room, where a short man was bent nearly double, clawing mushrooms with long fingers. He looked like a machine made for the job.

"How do I get out of here?" Brace said.

"Lunchtime."

"Which way is out?"

"Lunchtime."

"Uh, where's the boss man at?"

In one smooth motion, without standing or breaking rhythm, the man pointed in the direction Brace had come. Brace walked back, a sense of panic growing in him, uncertain if he was headed toward daylight or deeper into the blackness. Looming ahead was the immense shadow of the tall man he'd met earlier. The man smiled and waved. Rounding one last corner, Brace saw a rectangle of light that marked the entrance. He ran the rest of the way, stumbled onto the packed dirt parking lot, and sprawled in the grass. A short woman approached him holding a bucket of water and a dipper gourd.

"Here," she said.

He washed as best he could. The woman watched him closely.

"You a Gifford?" she said.

"Yeah, Brace."

"Lily's boy?"

He nodded.

"What are you doing here?" she said.

"Nothing, I don't reckon. I just quit."

"Son," she said, "you ort not be working here a-tall."

"I'm old enough."

"Ain't that," she said. "All the pickers are slow-minded. Not a one finished grade school."

Brace sat in the grass and let the information wash over him as if dumped by the long-stemmed gourd. No wonder the boss had repeated his instructions so often. Brace began laughing, and the woman joined him. She asked if he could drive, then suggested he fill in for a man who hadn't shown up. For the next two years, he'd delivered mushrooms.

The vast panorama of recollection faded abruptly, and Brace realized he was sitting on the porch swing with his beloved grand-niece and a stranger, perhaps her latest beau. In the yard below the maple, a second fledgling was flopping awkwardly on the dirt. Brace had missed its departure from the nest. He shrugged inwardly—there were two more baby birds to go, and he knew he'd see one. At least he'd stopped talking before telling the horrendous reason he'd quit driving the week after his eighteenth birthday.

"Uncle Robin," Sandra said, "are you thirsty? I'm going to get us all some water. You still off coffee?"

"Yeah," Brace said. "I gave it up. Made me jittery watching birds."

The swing swayed as she stood and entered the house, the screen door banging twice, then a third time softly. He needed to replace the spring. He'd get to it when the fledglings learned to fly.

"Pretty good job," Mick said. "A young guy out driving around."

"Yeah, I seen the world. Much of it as I wanted to, anyway."

"Vietnam must have been going on back then."

"Was. I had a high number. Then it was over."

"You must've known the quarry pretty good."

"The front part, I did. They's miles of rooms. I never went too far in after I started driving. Never had no need to."

"If you was to hide something, say a suitcase, where would a good place be?"

"The front. There was little places carved in the walls. One had a metal cabinet with two drawers for accounts. Paper had to be close to the mouth on account of the damp. That place was wetter than the inside of a creek."

Sandra returned with cups of water. She joined her great-uncle on the swing.

"I found your eyeglasses," she said.

"Wondered where they were at."

"They were sticking out of the toaster."

"Reckon I forgot to look there."

She frowned with concern.

"How do you see without them?" she said.

"They're drugstore cheaters," he said. "I see good far away. It's the up close that's tough. Reading and such."

"How about I tidy up in there?" she said. "Won't take a minute."

"No need, Little Sandy. But thank ye."

The sun began its slow descent behind the western slopes. The tree line along the top looked like golden fringe. The long dark shadow of the hill lay over the land, moving closer. A mockingbird began its polyglot call.

"That's my favorite bird," Mick said.

"It's a good one," Brace said. "Blue eggs, speckled. Three or four at a time. They favor a low bush. Some years they use the same nest."

"Were you there when the mushrooms went out of business?" Mick said.

Brace nodded.

"I hear there's a story to it," Mick said. "Satanists or whatnot."

"Naw, that was just something folks said later."

"Uh-huh. Why's that?"

Brace looked long and hard at the stranger, opening his forest-honed perceptions to the possibility of trust. He hadn't talked to anyone in two weeks and didn't mind it. If his niece had confidence in the man, maybe Brace should, too.

"Little Sandy," Brace said. "Reckon it wouldn't hurt if you helped out in the house a little. Might could use it."

"It just might," she said.

Sandra stood, giving Mick a quizzical glance, and went inside. A minute later Brace could hear the kitchen radio. He briefly recalled the small transistor radio that dangled from the rearview mirror during his delivery runs. It was a Zenith, black with silver trim. He carried spare batteries in the glove box. At night he tuned in to WLS out of Chicago and listened to music considered outrageous and devilish in the hills. Brace wondered what became of the radio. Maybe it was in the house. The stranger's voice snapped his mind to focus.

"Why'd they quit selling mushrooms?" Mick said.

"It was bad."

"I heard business was good."

"The reason they shut down was bad, real bad."

"Can you tell me what happened?"

"Mushrooms was selling like crazy. They hired more pickers, then a new guy to boss them inside. On weekends women brought their kids with them to buy mushrooms. The new picker boss started telling kids there was a room in the back filled with toys. At first nobody thought nothing of it. Just a feller being nice to kids. Then word got out he took a girl back there. Nobody believed it, but then it happened again, three or four times. It wasn't nothing anybody wanted to talk about. What he was doing to them girls."

"They go to the law over it?"

"Not back then. One girl's daddy beat the tar out of a picker but got the wrong man. Another feller said he'd shoot the manager. He quit, and the delivery boss quit, and the short lady, too. The whole operation fizzled out. I got on with a road crew building the new interstate. That lasted me till it was done. Saved every nickel and been right here ever since."

"What about the guy messing with the kids?" Mick said.

"Disappeared. Nobody ever saw him again."

Brace watched the fledglings. One walked in a circle and tipped over. The talking had tired him. His niece's car was in the yard, but he didn't know where she was. Had the stranger stolen her car?

"Who are you again?" Brace said.

"I work with Sandra."

"She's a dispatcher with the county."

"My sister's sheriff."

"Where is she?"

"In court."

"Little Sandy's in court? I don't believe you. She's as good-hearted as they get."

"My sister's in court, Mr. Gifford. Your niece is in the house. Let me go get her."

"Stay out of my house."

Mick nodded.

"Sandra," he yelled. "Your uncle's wanting you to come out here."

A few seconds passed, and she emerged from the house, wiping wet hands on a towel.

"You need you an apron, Uncle Robin," she said.

Brace lifted his chin to indicate Mick.

"This feller with you?" he said.

"Yes, he is. He's all right. He's helping us out. He's a Hardin."

"I knowed Hardins."

"Jimmy was my dad," Mick said.

"Homer Jack your papaw?"

Mick nodded.

"He was right handy in the woods," Brace said. "Quiet as a mouse and could see like a bat."

Mick stood and walked to the edge of the porch.

"I'll wait in the car," he said to Sandra.

"Watch and don't scare my babies," Brace said.

Mick left the porch and walked a wide arc to avoid the birds. They appeared to be resting from exertion. Sandra talked to her great-uncle for several minutes, went in the house, and returned with a plate of food. Mick watched them eat. Half an hour later, she joined him in the car, her face angry.

"What'd you say to him?" she said. "He's upset."

Mick shook his head. She started the car and drove along the old road, waving to her uncle.

On the porch Brace lifted his arm briefly in farewell,
then switched his attention to the fledglings. One gave a little hop as if testing gravity. Everything he told the stranger
was true, but only a few people knew the part he didn't tell.
Four men had captured the boss picker and driven him to
the quarry. One man stayed with the truck as lookout while
the other three dragged the picker deep underground. They
pressed his face into the manure until he suffocated. They
left the body and walked out of the quarry. Brace had been
the lookout waiting in the truck.

Chapter Fifteen

Lawton was an abandoned town with a state highway that ran through its center. Mick drove along 174, a route with various names including the Main Road, the Haldeman Road, the Old Road, and the Lawton Road. He passed abandoned stores, the remnants of a railroad station, and empty homes with collapsing roofs. A few wood-frame houses had gravel driveways and well-trimmed yards.

Behind the railroad bed he followed a road up a hill to the Mushroom Mines. The quality of the road surprised him. It had been resurfaced and widened to allow dual passage. He stopped to examine the blacktop, which was fortified for heavy traffic. The work was fresh. He listened and heard nothing except a male bobolink calling in mid-flight. Mick watched it land on a sycamore and jerk its head about as if trying to readjust its white cap. A large box truck descended the hill, straining in first gear. There was no business logo on the doors or side panels. The license plate was obscured by mud in a way that appeared deliberate.

Mick removed his pistol from the glove box and walked through the woods parallel to the road, wondering if the box truck had picked up cargo or made a delivery. Mick skirted a thicket of wild blackberry with thorny strands higher than his head. He circled deeper into the woods and arrived at the tree line, which bordered an expanse of fresh cement, big enough for the truck to turn around.

The rest of the ground was overgrown by sapling, weed, and bush. A pile of gravel had tall fescue growing from it. Beyond it were the remnants of an abandoned construction project that was at least a decade old. Three buildings had been started. A more advanced undertaking featured a foundation with four walls, an entry, openings for windows, and four concrete steps. None of the structures had a roof or door. Their unfinished barrenness had a forlorn quality, as if the buildings had been practice before the crew moved on to more substantial work.

Behind the ruins was a high rock cliff topped with dirt and forest, over which a Cooper's hawk drifted on a thermal in the crisp blue sky. Cut into the cliff was an opening large enough to accommodate a Bradley tank. The edges had been mended with fresh concrete block. Motion in Mick's peripheral vision caused him to retreat into the heavy shadows of the woods. A man walked the perimeter carrying a pistol on his hip. He wore boots and jeans, a ball cap with a silver insignia, and a polyester tactical jacket. He patrolled in the ungainly fashion of a big man more comfortable in the weight room of a gym than outdoors. Mick eased deeper into the woods and spent a half hour circling the site. He saw a Jeep, two pickup trucks, a camper van, and three more armed men. One was smoking a cigarette near the road.

Mick walked back through the woods, nodding casually to a multicolored hognose snake sunning itself on a rock. He'd been a kid the first time he encountered one, known as a "blow viper" because of its warning hiss. It had struck at his leg, startling him. Later his grandfather explained that hognoses weren't dangerous but were expert head-butters. Mick left the woods and strode toward the smoking man. He snapped his cigarette away and squared himself to look tough. Mick smiled and spread a thick accent over his voice.

"Y'all hiring?" he said. "Heard they was work up here for a man willing to work. I'm that man."

"Who the fuck are you?"

"I'm a Hardin. I'll work all day for a man that pays."

"There's no jobs here."

"They's something going on. We seen the trucks and all."

The man walked toward Mick. He was mid-thirties, with the fit body and hard glare of a combat veteran.

"How'd you get up here?" he said. "I don't see a car and didn't hear one."

"Come through the woods. Big bunch faster than using them old roads. I'll do ever what you want done. You pay cash, and I ain't picky."

"This is private property. You need to leave."

The man reached for his revolver, but Mick was quicker. He aimed the Beretta at the man's chest. The man cocked his head as if surprised and moved his hand away from his holster.

"A Beretta M9," he said. "Where'd you serve?"

"I'm leaving. Any one of those other men fires a shot, you're the first to die."

The man grinned in admiration.

"Hold off, boys," he yelled. "Let him get into the woods."

Mick walked backward to the road, crossed it quickly, and entered the safety of the trees. Three bursts of automatic gunfire shredded the leaves above his head. He dropped to the ground, rolled behind an oak, and quick-crawled across the forest floor until the slope of the hill blocked the bullets. He stood and ran to his truck, climbed inside, and started the engine. He headed downhill, taking more fire. The side mirror exploded. He sped to the blacktop, wrenched the wheel onto 174, swerved to avoid a dog, and kept the accelerator to the floor for several miles. At the first wide spot, he pulled onto a dirt road, turned the truck around, and opened both doors. To anyone following him, it would appear as if two men were hiding behind the doors. He stepped into the woods beside the truck. For thirty minutes he waited, calming his body by breathing deeply. Satisfied that he was alone, he drove slowly to Rocksalt.

At Linda's house he showered the dirt and sweat off his body, wondering what he'd stumbled into. As he dried himself, he wished he hadn't mentioned his own last name.

Chapter Sixteen

As a private citizen, Linda wanted to attend the memorial service for Mason. But she knew her presence would remind people that nobody had been arrested for the murders, which might affect her campaign. She hated thinking that way, letting politics influence her decisions. Still, Linda was pragmatic, she assigned Johnny Boy to the funeral home. His fear of ghosts would be mollified by the presence of all the living people.

Mick parked his truck at the edge of the funeral home parking lot with a view of the front door, propped open in welcome. Two men stepped outside and lit cigarettes. Wind blew the smoke back inside. Mick considered the sad fact that even with two recent dead, the Kissick family couldn't get a break from the slightest breeze.

In the past two days he'd performed online research on the Mushroom Mines. As Johnny Boy said, Mega Mountain had been purchased recently, but it was impossible to track down the owner. Even with his limited internet skills, Mick understood that the trail led to shell companies owned by shell companies. He couldn't figure what was worth the level of security he'd encountered. Chemical weapons. Gold bullion. Human trafficking. A dirty bomb. Money laundering. None of it quite made sense. Every option needed more versatile access than one road from a ghost town in the hills. Maybe it was high-tech data storage after all.

People began leaving the funeral home. After the first wave of departures, Johnny Boy came outside and walked to the truck.

"What happened to your mirror?" he said.

"Backed into a tree," Mick said. "How was it in there?"

"Bad."

"Looked like what, thirty people?"

"Something like that," Johnny Boy said. "They're a small family."

"Any strangers there?"

"I knew everybody except that Kissick boy in from California. He's a tough-looking son of a buck."

Mick nodded.

"Funeral's for family only," Johnny Boy said. "They's some folks headed to the house after."

"I'll go," Mick said. "You did your part."

He reached into a paper sack on the bench seat and handed Johnny Boy a bottle of Dr Pepper.

"Oh man," Johnny Boy said, "I need one right now. Can't believe you remembered."

Mick opened the truck door and Johnny Boy used the latch to snap the cap off the bottle. He drank a third of the contents, his Adam's apple pumping like a bobber on a fishing line.

"I got to go," he said. "Bunch of paperwork over that graffiti at the lake. A man filed charges. Fred White, goes by Porky."

"For graffiti? What was it?"

"Somebody spray-painted 'Porky White Sucks Big Green Donkey Dicks.'"

"That'll be some fun paperwork."

Johnny Boy flashed him the swiftest grin in the county, something he was known for—that and his lack of humor. He drank another third of the Dr Pepper, then looked at the bottle.

"Just enough left for some peanuts. I got a bag at the office. Thanks, Mick."

Mick drove out of the lot with a couple of hours to kill before visiting the Kissick family. He went to the IGA and bought small red potatoes, celery, onion, and half a carton of eggs. His grandfather had taught him a few rudimentary recipes that emphasized breakfast. The old man's single specialty was potato salad, good for any social occasion. It was easy to make, cheap, and wouldn't spill during transport.

At his sister's house he boiled the potatoes with a little salt then rinsed them with cold tap water. While the eggs boiled, he chopped the celery and onion, rummaged the refrigerator for milk and mayonnaise. There were no pickles. After combining the ingredients in a bowl, he covered it with aluminum foil, then headed to the edge of the county.

He stopped at the Rocksalt city limits and parked in an empty lot. Something had been gnawing at him for a couple of days, a wisp of a feeling just beyond the perimeter of his perception, intangible and swiftly retreating. Sudden awareness draped over him like a steel shawl—he was lonely. The depth of the sensation surprised him. He was accustomed to living alone, traveling alone, and working alone. He talked to his sister, listening mainly, which he supposed counted as human contact if not an actual conversation. He loved his sister. She loved him, but his presence in her house was an intrusion, and they tried to give each other plenty of latitude. He'd even taken to lowering the commode lid like she preferred, something he'd never done with his wife. Maybe he should have. Maybe they'd still be together. He shook his head at his own thoughts—Peggy had gotten restless due to his prolonged deployments and had an affair. It was understandable, even acceptable in the long-term, but the pregnancy wasn't.

Lately at night he'd been thinking about Sandra, a bad idea. He was leaving in a week, and there was no sense getting mixed up with somebody here, let alone a woman who worked for his sister. Still, he had to admit that she was the first new woman in seventeen years to catch his attention. He didn't even know why, which perplexed him further.

He turned the truck around and drove through town to one of the newer streets, McCulloch, wondering if it was named for the chainsaw. He stopped at an older house, small and white, with bird feeders in the front yard and small tanks of sugar water for hummingbirds. He tightened his lips, wondering if he was making a mistake, then got out of his truck, walked along the flagstones to the front door, and knocked. A minute passed. He was about to knock again when the door opened, and Sandra stood with a stack of books in her hands.

"Hidy, Mick," she said. "Come on in."

She stepped aside, and he entered, fighting the impulse to offer to relieve her of the burden she carried.

"Have a seat," she said. "Let me put these up."

She walked down a hall. The front room was tidy in a way his sister's never was—a pale orange blanket draped over the back of the couch, three shelves of paperback novels, two framed prints of horses in a field painted in an expressive fashion, seven plants in the window, and sheer curtains tied back by ribbons attached to cup hooks. The floor held two easy chairs in front of a homemade ottoman made of large juice cans covered in floral fabric.

"Like that?" Sandra said. "My great-aunt makes them. If you want one, I've got a garage full."

"It's very nice," Mick said.

"Won't tip over and sturdy enough for a bigger man than you to stand on."

Mick nodded, abruptly unsure of what he was doing, how things had transpired that he was admiring a footstool in a civilian's house. He'd been right—it was an error.

"Uh," he said. "Maybe I should go."

She laughed, a sweet sound of genuine mirth.

"Do you need something?" she said.

"Uh, yeah. You got any pickles?"

"Yes, how many do you need?"

"I don't know. Enough for a potato salad."

"How much?"

"How much what?" he said.

"Potato salad, Mick. What's wrong with you?"

He went to the truck for the pink mixing bowl, his mother's, with its white pattern of corn and roosters on the side. He tightened the foil and carried it into the warmth of Sandra's home. She called from the kitchen, and he joined her, placing the bowl on the counter beside a jar of pickles, a knife, and a cutting board. She peeled back the foil and peered at the contents.

"Good work," she said. "Didn't peel the potatoes. They're a lot better that way."

She used a fork to take a small bite.

"Did you add vinegar?" she said.

"No. I thought it was for cleaning."

She laughed again, deftly diced a single pickle, and folded in the tiny chunks with a spatula. She added a capful of apple cider vinegar. After gently mixing it, she tried another bite, lifted her eyebrows at him, and sprinkled paprika over it. She gave him a clean fork. He tried a bite, and the difference from before was distinct.

"Thank you," he said.

"Did you come by for cooking lessons? Or to invite me to a picnic?"

"I don't know. Neither. I have to go to the Kissicks' for a gathering."

"They bury Mason today?"

Mick nodded.

"Well," she said, "not my go-to for a first date, but let me change."

Without waiting for a response, she left the kitchen. Mick covered the potato salad, put the supplies away, washed the knife and forks, and wiped down the cutting board. The kitchen had been recently renovated with a single large metal sink and a splash guard made of subway tile. A wind chime jingled outside a window. On the wall was a clock made to resemble Elvis Presley with his legs separate from his body. Sandra returned to the room.

"You like Elvis?" she said. "He used to dance when it ticked but it drove me nuts so I took the cog out."

"I never seen one before."

"Not everybody's into clocks."

"My mother was. She had about forty."

"No Elvis?"

"Mom said he looked like a hoodlum."

"Get the salad."

He obeyed and followed her to the front room, where she picked up a small purse on a long strap. Outside, she went to the passenger side of the truck and climbed in.

"Nice rig," she said. "A '64?"

"Sixty-three. You know trucks?"

"I like old Chevys. The only Ford I like was the Ranchero. Beat the heck out of the El Camino."

Mick nodded. He felt more comfortable driving, faced with a specific task that required his attention. They rode silently out of town and along the blacktop between the wooded hills. Walnut trees were still leafing out. He veered around a five-foot-long corn snake stretched in the warm sun along the road's edge. Mick wished his life was that simple.

"Most guys would have run over it," Sandra said.

Mick nodded.

"You like snakes?" she said.

"I don't have a favorite, if that's what you mean."

"Like this truck?"

"Not a favorite either. I drive it because it belonged to my papaw. He raised me. And snakes, they got a right to live same as any animal. He taught me that, too."

"You learned a lot from him."

"Yeah," Mick said, "except about vinegar."

He glanced at her smile, grateful for it.

"What'd he teach you about women?" Sandra said.

"Not enough."

"How to avoid a question for one thing, right?"

"Naw, I learned that in the army."

She laughed, and it occurred to Mick that she laughed often, and he enjoyed it. Most people didn't laugh enough, including him. He saw the world as absurd, which required a pragmatism that he put to direct use. It was failing him now.

"Papaw didn't know much about women," he said. "Be nice to them. Listen. Carry heavy things. Do outside work."

"While women did the inside work."

"Not exactly. It was just him and me mostly. My dad till I was ten. My great-grandpa for a while, too."

"What happened to the wives?"

"They died or left."

As they drove away from town, the road became closer to the hills, with no shoulder. A red-tailed hawk broke across the road, low and swift, flying into a natural gap in the trees. Mick slowed and saw a rabbit immobilize itself at the base of a staghorn sumac.

"See that rabbit?" he said.

"Missed it," she said. "I like rabbits. Always wondered how they get by. Their whole job is to get eaten. They can't fight, fly, or climb a tree. Their only defense an unpredictable hop. Then they hold still. It's a wonder they made it this long without going extinct."

"Big litters," Mick said. "They give birth every month."

"It's the only animal in North America that hops."

"Frogs. Grasshoppers. Bunch of spiders."

"Mammal, I mean," she said.

Mick made the turnoff to the Kissick road, where several vehicles were already parked—three in the yard and a few on the narrow shoulder. He went past the house, turned around, then drove past the line of cars and parked at the end. He got out of the truck and waited, in case Sandra wanted to carry the potato salad. As an uninvited guest, maybe she'd prefer to arrive with food. She left the truck and walked to his side.

"What's all this parking maneuver for?" she said.

"Old habit," he said. "Gave me a chance to look over the cars."

"See anything suspicious?"

"Not a thing. You want to carry the potato salad?"

"You made it, you tote it."

They crossed the yard together and entered the house. Shifty Kissick sat in the front room surrounded by women with sympathetic expressions. A few men stood against the walls and looked at the floor. Sandra walked straight to Shifty, bent from the waist, and hugged her. Mick went to the kitchen, nodding to a few people with the Kissick build and look. The married-ins were obvious by their height and pale complexions. The kitchen table held an array of food. Soup beans simmered on the stove. There were two iron skillets with fresh cornbread, containers of fruit salad, green beans, and a large metal tray of fried chicken. Several bags of chips were piled on a counter, undoubtedly brought by single men who'd stopped at a gas station on the way over.

Standing beside the refrigerator was a man staring at Mick, tense and alert. He was clearly a Kissick, but bigger than any of the other men, his shoulders broad, his arms long, his fingers tapered as if sculpted. He had wide hips and sturdy Kissick legs covered by loose cargo pants. He wore a tight black shirt that was styled like a T-shirt but looked more expensive. Thick muscle corded his forearms, covered by several tattoos. It was the Marine haircut, high and tight, that identified him as the last of Shifty's sons.

Mick set the potato salad on the table.

"I'm Mick," he said. "I knew your brothers."

"Raymond. You the cop helping Mom?"

"I'm helping her, but I'm not a cop. Army CID."

"Before that?" Raymond said.

"Hundred-and-First Airborne. Attached to the Fifth Special Forces Group."

"You out now?"

"No, medical leave. How about you? Still in?"

"Retired a year ago. Third Battalion."

"Trinity," Mick said. "How's the saying go? 'First Battalion makes men, Second makes Marines, Third makes machines.'"

Raymond shrugged, and Mick nodded.

"Where at?" Mick said.

"Here and there."

"Doing what?"

"This and that."

A long minute passed. Mick understood that Raymond had worked black, wearing no insignia, in hot zones under secret orders. Mick wondered how many weapons he was carrying.

"You find anything out?" Raymond said.

"A little. I think the same people killed both your brothers. You know about Barney's business?"

"Yeah. Mason wasn't part of it."

Someone entered the room, and Mick turned to see Sandra, with a smile on her face, hurrying across the linoleum.

"Ray-Ray," she said. "It's so good to see you."

They hugged tightly, and Mick wondered about their history.

"I'm so sorry for your family," she said. "Mason was the sweetest thing. I never knew Barney, but everybody says he was all right."

"You look the same as ever, Sandy. Beautiful."

"Aw, thanks. So do you."

"You coloring your hair yet?"

"I'll never tell," she said, and laughed. "I see you're coloring your arms."

"You ought to see my back."

She laughed again.

"How long are you in?" she said.

"Depends on what this army dog has to say. I hear you're working for the county."

"Yeah. Mick's sister is sheriff, my boss."

"Cozy."

"Small town," she said, "small county."

"Why I got out," Raymond said.

Mick left the room. He didn't know what to say to the other guests and abruptly wasn't sure why he'd come. He stepped into Shifty's field of vision, waited until she noticed him, and gave her a short nod. She tightened her mouth and turned to a child, a granddaughter he assumed, holding a paper plate with three brownies. One fell to the floor, and the girl looked around as if in fear of admonishment. Shifty gathered the child onto her lap and stroked her hair.

Mick went outside, where three men stood smoking cigarettes. One held a long-necked bottle of Ale-8.

"You're a Hardin, ain't you?" he said.

Mick nodded.

"Your sister here?"

Mick shook his head.

"She know who killed those boys yet?"

"No," Mick said. "She's trying. But no luck. Got any ideas? I'll tell her."

"No, I don't. Everybody liked Mason, only he didn't know it. Nobody liked Fuckin' Barney, and he didn't know that either. No reason to kill either one of them."

"There's never a reason," Mick said.

The men smoked and thought about that, looking at clumps of sedge in the field, last year's yellow mixed with fresh green fronds. A plump woodcock lifted from the ground with a worm trailing from its long beak.

"Damn," one of the men said. "Ain't seen a timber-doodle since I was little."

Another man withdrew a phone from his pocket and began rapidly scrolling. Mick expected to see the usual photo—a fresh-shot tom turkey, a buck with a big rack, or a dead snake stretched across a road for scale. Instead, he heard the tinny sound of a saxophone. The man passed his phone around. On it was a woodcock in full mating display, strutting and rocking as if dancing, to the song "Tequila" by The Champs. The men laughed and laughed.

"Wish I had some tequila right about now," one said.

"I got a half pint of J.W. Dant in the car."

"J.W. Don't, they ort to call it."

The men laughed again, and one walked to his car for the cheap bourbon. He unscrewed the cap, grinned, and threw it over his shoulder.

"Won't be needing that," he said.

They passed the bottle. Each took a long pull and tried to conceal his reaction to the harsh burn. Mick positioned himself to be last in line, then when it came near, he moved again, stepping to the edge of the field as if watching for the woodcock. He didn't want to drink but knew that an overt refusal would insult the men.

Sandra came outside, trailed by Raymond. She hugged all the men, ignoring their scent of smoke, whiskey, and sweat. She reserved her longest embrace for Raymond, then smiled at Mick.

"Reckon you're ready to book," she said.

Mick nodded.

"Ray-Ray," she said, "make sure and call me."

"All right," he said, then aimed his hard eyes at Mick. "We need to talk."

Mick nodded his understanding and walked down the road to his truck, glad to be away from the house, the people, and the temptation of bourbon. When he drank, it was all he wanted to do, and it was better not to start.

He drove along the road. Sandra sighed, slumping into her side of the broad bench seat. An old sheet covered the torn upholstery.

"It's so sad," she said. "Poor Mrs. Kissick."

"Is she kin?"

"No. I knew all those boys though. Grew up with them."

"You got some history with Raymond."

She sat up straight and gave him a sharp look combined with the hint of a smile he couldn't interpret.

"Yes, I do," she said. "What's it to you?"

"Nothing," he said quickly. "Don't matter."

"It must, or you wouldn't bring it up. I do believe you're jealous. Is that it?"

"Of what?" he said. "No. I just . . . I don't know."

"Did you know Ray-Ray before he left?"

"No," Mick said.

"Know why he left?"

"He joined the Marines."

"Yes and no. Yes, he joined up. But that's not the reason."

He continued driving, knowing she was waiting for him to ask but not wanting to give her the satisfaction. He realized she was right—he did feel a tinge of jealousy, and now he was behaving like a kid.

"What's the reason?" he said.

"Ray-Ray's gay."

Chapter Seventeen

Mick's grandfather woke him every morning for the long walk to school along a footpath through the misty woods. Winters were mild in the hills, but it often snowed heavily enough to transform the bare trees into a chandelier. He was late for school, lost in the snowy woods. Papaw was calling his name.

Mick awoke to his sister in a house robe. He was instantly alert.

"Mick," she said. "Mick. Get up. Get dressed."

He rose without thought and slid into his clothes, carefully laid out for rapid deployment, his side-zip boots at the ready. Linda was in the kitchen making coffee. Through the window, the top of the western hill was tinged with yellow as the light drizzled down the slope.

"Police called," she said. "There's a fire at Papaw's cabin."

Mick left the house and drove fast through town, ignoring stop signs and red lights, wondering how bad the fire was, how it got started. A mistake, he thought, all the way around. He'd blindly trusted a madman, who'd set fire to his grandfather's house. At the head of the holler he could smell the smoke, then see it, a dark column that dissipated over the ridgeline.

Parked at the top of the hill were a fire truck and a Grand Cherokee emblazoned with the fire department insignia. One man spoke on a walkie-talkie. Three more stood back from the remnants of Mick's cabin—four charred walls and nothing else. The roof had burned off, the doors, the window frames, and the three oak steps to the door. The smoldering walls released heat into the air.

The chief put his hand up in a gesture of halt.

"It's my place," Mick said.

"You Linda's brother?"

Mick nodded.

"I'm sorry, bub. Nothing we could do. Somebody seen the smoke and called the forest ranger, who notified us. Did you store anything flammable here?"

"No."

The chief took a deep breath, looked at the cabin, and spoke in a low voice.

"Was there someone staying here?"

"Yeah, Jacky Turner."

The chief shook his head, then gestured with his chin to the cabin.

"We thought it was you," he said.

"Dead?"

"Probably smoke inhalation. Wouldn't have felt anything."

"Any marks or wounds on the body?"

"Can't tell. There's not much of him left."

The wind shifted, blowing the smoke toward Mick, carrying the pungent scent of gasoline.

"You smell that?" Mick said.

"We think it was set. A lot of accelerant and some empty gas cans. It started hot. The old walls held on okay. But there's nothing left inside."

Mick looked at the blackened shell of his cabin, a box with no lid. Someone had tried to kill Mick and got Jacky instead. An ambulance from town eased up the hill, followed by Johnny Boy's personal vehicle. The EMTs conferred with the fire chief.

"Jacky?" Johnny Boy said.

"Dead," Mick said.

"Some damn invention of his that went sideways?"

"The chief said arson."

"Who would try to hurt him?"

"I believe it was me they were after."

Johnny Boy swung his fist. Mick saw the blow coming and leaned forward to decrease the impact against his face. He rocked back on his heels and waited for the next one. Johnny Boy dropped his arms and looked at the ground.

"Sorry, Mick."

"No need. Go see his folks. Linda'll be here in a minute. Let her take care of things. Don't do anything you'll regret."

Johnny Boy turned away, his eyes glistening with tears. Mick ignored him. It was time to box his feelings up and lock them deep inside like a vault. One bad thought always led to another. Mick preferred fury to mourning. The cabin was the last thing left from his past, a charred ruin.

He stepped into the woods and made a slow circle, looking for sign. Finding nothing, he increased the perimeter by four feet and walked it again, then twice more, at eight feet and at twenty. The undergrowth was intact, save for the bark of young trees gnawed by deer. The arsonists hadn't come through the woods. They'd arrived by road, already driven by him, the fire chief, Johnny Boy, and the ambulance. He walked it anyway, knowing it was fruitless—any tracks from the killers would be obliterated.

He returned to the top of the hill. More vehicles had arrived, including Linda's SUV. He watched two firemen carry a body bag, their boots smoking, faces running with sweat. Steam rose from their turnouts. They moved slowly, utilizing great care as they loaded the woefully small bag into the ambulance.

"Who's that?" Linda said.

"Johnny Boy's cousin, Jacky."

"Damn it to all, to son-of-a-bitching hell. Who did it?"

"Could be anybody. Kids were partying in there while I was gone."

She sniffed the air.

"Gasoline party? I doubt that. Somebody set this fire, and I bet you know who."

"Ain't for sure."

"Are you not telling me because I'm your sister? Or are you like all the rest of these sexist assholes around here?"

"Because you're the sheriff," he said.

"That's even more reason to tell me."

"I'm not your deputy anymore."

"You don't get it, you stubborn fool. Are you in danger? Is there anybody else who might get killed? As sheriff, I need to know that."

Mick nodded.

"You're right," he said. "I think it's payback against me."

"For what?"

"Getting too close to figuring out who killed the Kissicks."

"You need to goddam start talking."

"I don't know everything yet," he said. "When I do, I'll tell you."

"If you're not dead."

The ambulance rolled down the hill, moving more slowly than Mick thought possible, the driver undoubtedly trying to protect the cargo. Animals would stay away until the heat subsided, then they'd scavenge for food. Mick recalled his grandfather telling him that after a fire during the Great Depression, he'd picked through the ashes searching for nails to reuse.

He waited for Linda's anger to pass, then spoke gently.

"What now, Sis?" he said.

"I'll call the state police and request ATF. They investigate arson. I'll work with them on it. You need to stay away from the cabin."

"Okay," he said. "I'd keep Johnny Boy on a leash for a while. He might try and track down who it was."

"He wouldn't hurt a fly."

"He might. He's from the hills, same as me."

"And me."

"No, it's different."

"Why, because I'm a woman?"

"Because you're from town."

Mick got in his truck and drove off the hill, past the fire truck too heavy to make it up the dirt road. A few miles down the blacktop his phone chirped, and he pulled over to check the message—a text from Dr. Harker said she needed to see him. He headed to town, deliberately driving below the speed limit due to the seething rage that coursed through his body. At a gas station he bought a large coffee in a Styrofoam cup. For the first time in many years he underwent a wild urge for a cigarette. The last time had been after a firefight. Outnumbered five to one, his squad had battled for hours while engaged in a tactical withdrawal. Mick was the only survivor.

He drove to the college and checked the time—eight-fifteen. Campus was mostly empty except for a few student athletes scurrying to class and an occasional blue truck driven by maintenance workers. Mick entered the geology building and knocked on Dr. Harker's open door.

"Come in," she said.

She looked at Mick for several seconds, scrutinizing him like a specimen of earth beneath her microscope. When she spoke, her voice was gentle with compassion.

"Have a seat," she said. "Tell me what's wrong."

Mick eased into the guest chair, struggling with the impulse to tell her everything.

"Some bad news of a personal nature," he said. "What do you need to see me for?"

"I heard from my colleague in chemistry. He's on sabbatical so it took a few days. He analyzed the soil sample four times to double-check the result. Are you sure that dirt is from your victim's boots?"

"I scraped it off myself," he said. "Why?"

"It contains a significant amount of radium-226. A highly toxic chemical."

"Where does it come from?"

"My general understanding is that it's a waste by-product from hydraulic fracturing of shale."

"Fracking," Mick said. "That got popular after I was posted overseas."

"'Popular' might not be the best word. It's a way of extracting natural gas for energy. In a nutshell, it means using high pressure to force water and chemicals into underground shale. The shale fractures and the gas can be removed by pumps. The biggest drawback is flowback water. Toxic as hell. Can't drink it or shower in it or use it in your garden. They have to dispose of it."

Dr. Harker stopped talking with a flourish, as if delivering the finale to a lecture in class. She appeared to be waiting for questions from a more attentive student.

"How do they get rid of it?" Mick said.

"Different methods. Sometimes it's poured straight into an injection well. The most common way is radioactive filter socks. Large bags. Shaped rather like a condom. They're dumped illegally or shipped out of state. Contaminated equipment is an issue, too. The bigger problem is that there's no oversight, no federal monitoring of disposal."

"Where does your colleague think the dirt came from?"

"That's a good question," she said.

Mick nodded, recognizing the professorial technique of praising a student while giving herself time to formulate a response. His patience and diplomacy were wearing thin. Like a young officer straight out of ROTC, she'd be reluctant to admit her own ignorance. She surprised him.

"He doesn't know," she said. "And I don't either. Kentucky law forbids importing radioactive waste. But there's a landfill down in Estill County with two thousand tons of it beside an elementary school. Maybe your victim worked there. Truck drivers get exposed to it, especially if it's illegal transport."

"Not him. He was self-employed."

"Right, a drug dealer."

"Yes, and somebody killed his brother up Rodburn Holler three days ago. If I were you, I'd not mention this to anybody, and tell your colleague, too."

"Are we in danger?"

"Not if you stay quiet."

Mick rose suddenly, a quick motion that startled her. He went to the door, gathered a deep breath, and faced her again.

"I'm serious, Dr. Harker," he said. "Keep this to yourself. Get rid of that dirt and destroy any notes."

He walked outside, thinking about the radium-226 on Fuckin' Barney's boots. Maybe the truck he'd seen at the Mushroom Mines contained a delivery of toxic waste. Somebody was making a lot of money if they were willing to kill for it.

Chapter Eighteen

Shifty Kissick had slept in her recliner all night, exhausted from grief and the lorazepam she'd taken with whiskey after everyone left. Her sister had offered to stay the night, but Shifty sent her home. She felt safe with Ray-Ray. At dawn he'd helped her out of the chair to her bed. He was shirtless, and she'd decided not to mention the tattoos that covered his back like the inside of a comic book. Nothing mattered anymore. She curled beneath the blanket and cried herself to sleep like a child.

Raymond knocked out a hundred sit-ups, a hundred push-ups, and a hundred jumping jacks. Despite the exertion, he breathed easily. A slight perspiration coated his skin. He drank two glasses of water sweetened by a cherry tree his father had planted by the well forty years before. He did yoga to stretch his back, then searched the house. His mother had a cut-down .410 shotgun, a small .32 pistol, and a long-barreled .22 revolver. Personal guns, family guns. The shotgun was good for snake and not much else. He recalled his father hunting squirrels with the .22, aiming for the bark beside the squirrel's head. The shock of the bullet's impact stunned the animal enough to fall out of the tree. His dad called it "barking a squirrel." It was a way to get meat without much damage.

Raymond cleaned the weapons out of habit, knowing he'd need bigger firepower if the house came under attack. As a child, he hadn't liked Barney and barely knew Mason. They'd been kids when he enlisted in the Corps. He'd returned home twice, once after boot camp and the second time for his father's funeral. Encountering neighbors and family last night had been difficult—the same people had judged him in the past. Now they ignored him out of fear. The highlight had been seeing Sandra Caldwell, the only friend he'd had. As kids they'd confided their dreams, none of which included her working for the county or him in the Corps and his little brothers dead.

He went outside and began a tai chi routine with Warrior posture, then Part the Horse's Mane. Breathing deliberately, he moved with a barely perceptible slowness into Crane Spreads Wings. After twenty minutes, sweat was coursing down his torso and limbs. He transitioned into Golden Cock Stands on One Leg, gradually shifting from one foot to the other.

An old truck appeared on the road, traveling slowly, then stopped. Someone got out and stood beside the cab.

Raymond flowed into a final pose, inhaled deeply, and focused his vision on the man as he released a long exhale.

"Mick Hardin," Mick said. "We met the other day."

"Sergeant Potato Salad."

"You might be the first man in the county to ever do tai chi."

"You want coffee?"

Raymond went in the house and returned with two cups. Mick followed him to the backyard, and they sat in metal chairs with peeling paint, a tree stump between them as a table. There was a shed, a tire swing dangling from a hickory, and an empty chicken coop.

"Couple of years ago," Mick said, "your mom had a chicken that could walk backwards."

"Ol' Sparky. Something got him. Fox or hawk. Mommy never believed in penning animals up. Or us kids."

Mick nodded and sipped the strong coffee. Fifteen minutes later he'd told Raymond everything he knew about the Mushroom Mines, the chemical on Barney's boots, and the arson attack. Raymond listened without interruption. Mick finished his coffee and flung the dregs, which speckled the grass like the dark larvae of a soldier fly.

"Let me get this straight," Raymond said. "You think Barney hid his stash in the mines a while back. Then somebody started dumping toxic waste there. Barney went back for the stash, and they killed him, then moved his body to town. Mommy sent Mason, and they killed him, too. You went up there, and they tried to burn you out. On top of all that, the Detroit mob wants their money back."

"That's my working theory. I think those guys at the Mushroom Mines are ex-military, contractors working private."

"Why tell me?" Raymond said. "Tell your sister."

"Something like this she'd have to kick to the state police. The dope and toxic waste crossed state lines, which means the FBI gets involved."

"Why do you care? They're my brothers."

"A man staying at Papaw's cabin died because they thought he was me. I liked him. They killed him."

Raymond sat still for several minutes. Mick wondered if he was making a mistake by sharing the information. Raymond would want retribution. It was the code of the hills, one he tried to dissuade others from following, a path that could lead to bloodshed for generations, a path he was on himself. The men at the mines weren't local, which meant no danger of family vengeance. They were hired guns operating illegally and killing civilians. By the time federal authorities were mobilized to make arrests, the men would be long gone. He wondered if he was trying to talk himself into taking illegal action.

Raymond spoke in a soft voice, low and controlled.

"How many men did you see at the mines?" he said.

"Four."

"You good for one?"

Mick nodded.

"We'll need ordnance," Raymond said.

"Barney has some buddies with guns."

"He never had buddies."

"Business rivals. He worked something out. My opinion, they're armed to the teeth."

Raymond stood.

"Let's go," he said.

They drove silently to town in the truck and stopped at a bank, where Mick withdrew nine thousand dollars in hundreds. He headed east on Old US 60. Dawn had lifted like a veil. Sunlight streaming over the eastern hill threw a jagged shadow along the blacktop road, bisecting it with darkness and glare. A sudden wind exposed the velvety underside of leaves on a silver maple.

"Who we going to see?" Raymond said.

"Drug-dealer family. Rich Lange is the father, two boys that I saw. Way back up a hillside."

"Rough bunch?"

"As a cob."

"I don't know any Langes."

"I didn't either. They're just over the county line. Your brother made a turf deal with them on moving heroin."

Raymond sat easily against the old bench seat, posture erect, head turned slightly to see ahead and scan the ditch simultaneously. Mick recognized the vigilant stance of a man on military patrol. He was putting a lot of trust in Raymond based on nothing but instinct. He hoped it paid off.

"Are you with Sandy?" Raymond said.

"No. We've not even had a date. She went with me to your house, and we visited her uncle."

"Uncle Robin?"

Mick nodded.

"He was a crazy old coot twenty years ago," Raymond said.

"He's gone a little more down that road. I believe it's some kind of dementia."

"Still into birds?"

Mick nodded. He braked for a series of S curves that followed a creek, then accelerated on the brief straight stretch. Raymond rocked with the turns, remaining relaxed.

"Sandra tell you anything about me?" he said in a casual tone.

"A little. Your mom did, too."

"What'd Mommy say?"

"You stayed in California for a Mexican woman."

Raymond grinned.

"Mommy doesn't like Mexicans. Never met one, but her mind's made up. All Mexicans are bad. That kind of shit. I knew she wouldn't visit me if I was with a Latina."

Mick nodded.

"Fact is," Raymond said, "Mommy likes gay people even less than Mexicans."

"You used one bigotry against the other."

"Protecting her from herself."

"Sandra said that's why you enlisted," Mick said.

"Yes and no. I wanted out of these hills, same as you, probably. I picked the Marines because the dress uniform had a sword and a red stripe."

Mick laughed for the first time in days.

"You got a problem with me being gay?" Raymond said.

"No. All I care about is how you are under fire."

"I was thinking the same about you."

"I guess we'll both find out."

They drove in silence along the blacktop, turning onto narrower roads, then a single lane with no center stripe that ended at a dirt fork. Mick headed east up the steep hill to a ridge. Trees scraped against the mirror and door on the driver's side. The dirt road straightened to a wide spot, and Mick stopped.

"Around here," he said, "is where they picked me up last time."

"They know the truck?"

"No, but they know me."

Mick honked the horn twice, opened the door, and stepped out. He held his pistol high and set it on the hood. From the woods came a man in his thirties carrying a Bushmaster semiautomatic rifle with a folding stock and a high-capacity magazine. He wore a camouflage boonie hat, shirt,

trousers, and boots. A ten-inch Bowie knife hung in a scab-
bard tied to one leg. His belt held a holstered Glock and a
spare clip. Mick didn't recognize him.

"I'm Mick Hardin," Mick said. "Here to see Rich. He
knows me."

As before, the man relayed the message via cell phone,
listened to the response, then spoke.

"Who's the other boy with you?"

"Fuckin' Barney's brother."

"Ain't they all dead?"

"Not the oldest one. Raymond."

The man smirked and spat.

"I heard about him."

"We both need to come in. Tell Rich for me."

The man waited long enough to indicate that he didn't
follow orders from Mick, then muttered into the phone. He
grimaced and shook his head.

"All right," he said. "Either one of you got ary a gun
on you?"

Mick shook his head. Raymond got out of the truck,
lifted his shirt, and slowly turned in a circle. Mick moved
forward, and the man used his rifle to point up the hill. It
was a tactical error. Mick was close enough to step inside the
range of fire and dispatch the man. Mick glanced at Raymond to see if he noticed the mistake. Raymond grunted
and gave a nearly imperceptible frown.

They preceded the man up the hill. Strands of sunlight streamed through the canopy of oak and walnut,

illuminating the ferns and moss. A woodpecker climbed a trunk like a lineman scaling a telephone pole.

Rich Lange waited on the porch while his two sons stood in the yard. All were armed.

"Hidy, Mr. Lange," Mick said.

"What are you wanting now?"

"A little help."

"Done give it once."

"I know it. And I appreciate it. This time, I'm willing to pay you."

"Who's your buddy?"

Raymond took a step forward.

"Raymond Kissick. I'm Shifty's oldest boy."

The sentry in camouflage lifted his rifle.

"Lower that goddam gun, Peanut," Rich said. "You shoot, and the round'll go through him and into me or the house, one."

"Yes, sir," Peanut said. "Just that I know about Ray-Ray here. He's got a funny turn. Likes the brown-eye. I ain't of a mind to let him get too close. Can't trust a faggot."

No one spoke. Mick could feel the tension coming off Raymond in waves. The Lange sons were impassive, but the father narrowed his eyes in a hard glare at Peanut, who lifted his chin in defiance. Mick turned slightly to keep everyone in sight.

"Is Peanut one of your sons?" Mick said.

"No," Rich said. "He knocked my daughter up and married her three months ago."

"So he ain't blood."

"Not one speck."

Both Lange sons tightened their focus on Mick, inter-ested in the abrupt shift of conversation. Raymond didn't move. His eyelids had dropped to half-mast, and it was impossible to know what he was looking at. He could have been asleep.

"Hey, now," Peanut said. "I'm looking out for all of us. These queers'll come around on you and make a play for your wang."

"Mr. Lange," Mick said, "can you hush him up so we can do business."

"I can't do nothing with him," Rich said. "Maybe you can."

Mick looked at Raymond and tipped his head toward Peanut. A few seconds passed during which a chickadee called. Raymond sprang forward as if launched and grabbed the rifle barrel. He twisted it down and away, then chopped a single blow to Peanut's trigger hand. Peanut released the rifle, and Raymond tossed it behind him. Using both hands, he snatched the pistol from Peanut's belt and withdrew the Bowie knife.

"If you want to fight," he said, "I'll set the gun and knife down."

"You broke my fucking finger," Peanut said.

"I'll put one hand behind my back to make it even. You can have the first punch."

Peanut frowned, wondering if it was a trick. Mick almost felt sorry for him and hoped he'd back down. Peanut glanced at his brothers-in-law, who were grinning, and Mick knew the humiliation would overpower common sense. Peanut nodded to Raymond and stood.

Raymond set the weapons in the grass, moved his right arm behind his back, and tucked his hand inside his belt. He held his left arm at his side. Peanut charged with a roundhouse blow, which Raymond dodged easily. Peanut's momentum carried him forward, and he stumbled, then turned back and swung again. Raymond shifted his body, and the fist missed his face. He circled to his right, waiting for the next attack, expecting a clumsy feint. Sure enough, Peanut moved in with his right fist tapping the air, then pivoted to drive his left into Raymond's body, but Raymond had already spun away.

"You can quit now," Raymond said.

"You stop that karate shit, and I'll think about it."

"All right," Raymond said. "I'll just stand here then."

"You swear?"

"I could, but you won't believe me. You said you can't trust a faggot."

"Fuck you."

"No, thanks," Raymond said. "Either give up or come on."

"You really ain't going to move?"

Raymond stomped one boot at a time against the earth as if planting himself in place.

"I'll stay right here," he said.

"You heard him," Peanut said to his brothers-in-law. "He said he ain't moving."

They nodded. Peanut charged close, and Raymond struck a quick uppercut to the chin. Peanut dropped to the dirt on his back, arms splayed. He regained consciousness in a few seconds. Raymond helped him sit and examined his hand. He looked at Rich.

"It's a stable fracture," Raymond said. "Tape that finger to the middle one for a couple of weeks. He'll be all right."

Raymond retrieved the rifle and pistol, released both clips, and set the weapons on the ground beneath a maple. He placed the Bowie knife beside them.

"Mr. Lange," Mick said. "We got a line on who killed Fuckin' Barney and Mason. We need some weapons."

"Go to the store. Background check takes ten minutes."

"I don't want an official record of the sale."

"Because of what you got in mind?"

Mick nodded.

"No dice," Rich said.

"Why's that?"

"You go up against somebody, and they find out where you got the guns, I'll have one more enemy."

"You don't know them," Mick said. "They're not in the dope business."

"What's their trade?"

"I believe it's illegal disposal of toxic waste."

"You ain't for sure?"

"We need guns to find out."

"Here in Elliott County?"

Mick shook his head.

"No skin off my ass," Rich said.

"It's right on the county line," Mick said. "It's all our asses if that shit gets in the drinking water."

"That bad?"

"Bad enough to kill three men for, yeah."

"Who was the third?"

"Jacky Turner. He was staying at my papaw's cabin when they burnt it down."

"Thought he was you?"

Mick nodded. Rich scratched his beard and readjusted his ball cap, gestures that Mick knew gave him time to think. The morning sun illuminated a long, ragged strip of cloud bisected by the contrail of a jet.

"When I was a boy," Rich said, "them jets used to make sonic booms. Big loud sound that hushed the woods. It'd rattle the window glass and knock a shingle off a roof. I don't hear them anymore."

"They got banned in the seventies," Mick said.

"How do you ban a noise?"

"You can't," Raymond said. "What they did was stop supersonic jets from flying over land. That plane up there is slower. What they call 'subsonic.' Doesn't break the sound barrier."

"You an air force man?" Rich said.

"No, sir."

"You're damn sure something."

Raymond shrugged without speaking. Refusing to answer the implied question was a good sign, but Mick wanted to avoid another conflict.

"Mr. Lange," he said, "we need to buy two assault-style rifles, two semiautomatic pistols, and spare ammo. You think you could help us?"

"Yep," Rich said. "Anything else?"

"Couple of chest rigs. Two sets of comms with tactical earbuds. Holsters. Flash-bang grenades."

"No flash-bangs."

"What about hand grenades?" Raymond said.

"None to spare," Rich said. "All this is going to run you a pretty penny."

"How much?" Mick said.

"How much you got?"

Mick watched the jet streamer dissipate into a long gray feather against the blue. He didn't want to waste time with negotiation. Rich had all the leverage. The sooner they were done, the better.

"I've got nine grand," Mick said.

Rich grinned, and the years fled his face. He suddenly resembled his sons.

"Lord love a duck," he said. "You ort to told me that a half hour ago. Might've saved Peanut a beatdown."

He looked at his sons.

"Boys," he said. "One of you take Peanut in the house and tape his fingers up. The other show Hardin what we got. I aim to talk to this Kissick."

The younger son dragged Peanut to his feet and escorted him up the steps and into the house. Mick joined the older Lange brother. Raymond watched them until they were out of sight. A dog barked, then another, the sound coming from behind the house.

"You sure about Peanut's finger?" Rich said.

"Yeah. Break it wrong, and it's a mess. Do it right, it'll heal up. I did it right."

"Where'd you learn that?"

Raymond shrugged.

"Fuckin' Barney was all right," Rich said. "You fixing to pick up where he left off?"

"No, sir."

"What is it you want?"

"Set things straight."

"Is it true what Peanut said about you?" Rich said.

"No, sir. I'm very trustworthy."

"I didn't mean that part."

A gray-and-yellow meadowlark landed on a fence post and looked about with his shoulders hunched. After a few seconds he stretched his neck and emitted a three-note rising call. Neither man spoke. Rich moved to a chair and sat.

"I understand why you're here," Rich said. "Family. But how'd that Hardin boy get mixed up with this?"

"I wondered that myself."

"Y'all ain't buddies?"

"I met him two days ago."

Mick and Rich's older son circled the house carrying weapons and gear. They laid everything out on the porch steps like goods at a bake sale. Mick pulled a stack of hundreds from his pocket. He passed the money to the Lange son, who counted it, then nodded to his father.

"Before you go," Rich said, "you need to tell me why you're doing this."

"My papaw built that cabin. I grew up in it."

"Naw, you were up here before it burnt down."

"I told you then."

"You can tell me again, bub," Rich said. "Unless there's some reason you're keeping it to yourself. Like maybe you plan on taking over Fuckin' Barney's business."

"I already got a job."

"Soldier pay ain't much."

"You're right about that," Mick said. "Mrs. Kissick asked me to find out who killed her son."

"That's all it took?"

Mick nodded.

"She paying you?"

"She ain't got no money."

"You're crazy," Rich said. "But my kind. Go on and get, both of you."

Raymond and Mick carried the gear down the road to the truck. They stopped twice to check if they were followed. Nobody was there except a buzzard circling high in the sky as if waiting for something to die. A pair of sparrows flew through a narrow opening between the trees.

"Nine grand," Raymond said. "You got skinned alive."

"I know it. I just wanted off that hillside."

"Why'd you bring that particular amount?"

"Patriot Act. If you withdraw ten thousand, the bank has to report it to the IRS."

"Now what?" Raymond said.

"I got a personal errand to run."

"All right. Drop me at Mommy's. I'll clean the weapons and check the equipment."

They drove in silence off the hill to the blacktop, crossed the meat of the county, and headed up the dirt road to the Kissick home place. They carried the gear inside. Mick nodded once to Raymond and left.

Chapter Nineteen

At Linda's house Mick removed the divorce papers from his suitcase and spread three copies on the kitchen table. The language was simple, the document short. Peggy received three-quarters of their savings in exchange for leaving his eventual army pension alone. The only assets were the house in town, the truck, and the cabin. He'd agreed to swap the house for the cabin, a deal that was lopsided at the time, worse now with the cabin burned down. He stared at the official papers for a long time. The finality of it bothered him. The simple act of writing his name would erase a significant part of his life.

Each page had small stickers with arrows pointing to the spaces that required his signature. He supposed it was intended to be helpful, but Mick felt resentment, as if required to follow orders from the paper itself. He was signing copies when his sister entered the house through the kitchen door. Linda opened her mouth to speak, saw what he was doing, and clamped her lips tight as tendon to bone.

Mick finished and slid the original and one copy into an envelope.

"Do you need stamps?" she said. "There's some in the junk drawer."

"Same place Mom kept them," Mick said.

"Some things never change."

"Yeah, well . . . I guess me and Peggy did."

"If she used a Rocksalt lawyer, I can drop them off."

"I'll give them to her in person."

"You think that's a good idea?"

"Probably not. But it seems like the right thing to do."

She left the room and returned carrying a carton of signs that said VOTE HARDIN with a color photograph of her in uniform. They were bigger than her previous signs, higher quality.

"I heard from my cop buddy in Lexington," she said. "He recognized the yellow crowns on the heroin packets. Said they're all over the metro area. He traced them to a mid-level dealer in Frankfort. Thing is, he's sitting in jail right now."

"How long's he been in?"

"Three months. Could be somebody's taking over and expanding his territory."

"A few yellow crowns in Rocksalt isn't much of an expansion."

"Why do you do that?" she said. "Every damn time. You dispute what I say, then pick at it. I get enough of that from the mayor. Half the time he asks a question just to argue with the answer."

"I don't mean to, Sis. It's how I think. Trying to get to the bottom of things."

"Just stick with the damn top first. That's Frankfort heroin in Rocksalt. Somebody's bringing it in. There'll be more."

Mick nodded. Linda had a point—he had a tendency to peck at the ground like a chicken, until the grass was gone and he was stuck with rock and dirt. Facts revealed themselves eventually, but it was wrong to use his sister as the pecking ground.

"What do you think the crown means?" he said

"Could be anything. Rolex. Hallmark. Corona beer. Maybe somebody likes RC Cola."

"You've put thought to it."

"It's my damn job," she said.

She went to the kitchen door, which Mick quickly opened for her. She carried the box of signs to the carport, opened the hatch, and put it in the back of the SUV.

"Pretty fancy signs," he said.

"Yeah, I've got volunteers sticking them by voting houses and gas stations. Sort of a last-minute reminder."

"Election's tomorrow?" he said.

"Yes, damn it. You'd know if you paid attention to anything but your ownself."

"Uh-huh," Mick said. "I can set some signs out on the way to Owingsville."

"That's precinct two," she said. "I got that covered."

"I'm trying to help, Sis."

"You're a day late and a dollar short. As usual."

Mick let it go. She was nervous about the election, and he was a safe recipient of her anxiety. He figured Johnny Boy was avoiding her. It occurred to him that he was avoiding Sandra.

"One thing," he said. "I resign as deputy."

"Accepted."

"You need to let the city police know, too. They were there when you deputized me."

"It's not their business."

"No, and you don't want it to be."

She slammed the hatch on the back of her SUV and regarded him with a hard glare.

"What are you up to?" she said.

Mick didn't answer.

"Is this about Papaw's cabin?" she said.

"It's about the sheriff being formally distant from her brother."

"Formally?"

"You know what I mean, Sis. It's best if you tell those cops I'm not associated with your office anymore."

"I don't like the sound of this."

"What you don't like is the not knowing. Same as the election."

She nodded, then abruptly halted the movement of her head.

"Now you've got me doing that," she said. "You know I always hated your nodding. You and Papaw in the same room was nothing but nods."

"It's how we communicated."

"I like old-fashioned language."

"With cussing," he said.

"Fuck, yeah. Cussing makes you live longer. Did you know that? It gets shit out of your system."

"You'll live to a hundred and ten."

She smiled. The expression softened the tension in her face.

"Whatever you do," he said, "don't nod."

She laughed, and he felt grateful, as if he'd done his duty. He'd been able to make his sister laugh since they were kids. Nobody else could.

"I got to go," she said.

"Good luck tomorrow. You'll win."

Her expression hardened again. She got in her car, backed out of the driveway, and drove down Lyons Avenue. With Peggy out of his life, Mick was down to his sister for family. All the rest were long dead, except for a few cousins he hadn't seen in years. He wished he and Linda were closer but didn't know how to do it. Maybe that was why Peggy had left him.

At the edge of town he stopped for gas and headed west on Old US 60. He passed the turnoff to Lakeview

Heights, an upscale subdivision with no lake in sight. A few miles farther he drove through the community of Farmers, crossed the Licking River, and parked on the shoulder beside one of his sister's campaign signs. It was crooked from a bent leg. He straightened the wire and pushed it firmly into the earth. A car went by. The driver lifted his forefinger off the steering wheel, and Mick wondered if the man was waving to him, the old truck, or his sister's sign. Regardless, he jerked his chin in acknowledgment. Two country men following old codes with the bare minimum of motion.

Mick drove a few miles more and stopped at Zimmy's Quick Stop for a bottle of Ale-8. The land was a little flatter, which meant more farming, and he wondered how his life would be if his great-grandfather had settled here instead of deep in the hills. It was an old habit that he tried not to indulge, imagining his way into a life other than his own—a farmer, a storekeeper, a lawyer, a doctor. Instead, he was on his way to being an army lifer, an outcome he'd never wanted. Put in four years and go to college. Put in thirty and never fit in anywhere as a civilian. Maybe it was time to get out. In two years he'd have his twenty and could open a marina on Cave Run Lake. He'd sunburn himself to the grave.

He realized he was ruminating this way to avoid thinking about his errand. The last time he'd seen Peggy, she'd just given birth and was doped up in the hospital. That was a year ago. She'd texted once, when she heard he'd

204

CHRIS OFFUTT

been wounded. He wanted to see her, but at the same time he didn't. No matter how she looked, he saw the young woman he'd met seventeen years before, quick-witted and curious, loving and smart. She had a spontaneity he liked, a quality absent in himself. She was always ready to drop everything and go anywhere, but all the far she'd gotten was twenty-five miles from home.

He entered Owingsville and stopped. The divorce papers held Peggy's address, which he typed into the GPS on his phone. He was less than a quarter mile away. He had an impulse to turn around, drive to the Lexington airport, and return to Germany. His leg was healed. He could go back to work.

He put the truck in gear and drove to the address. Owingsville was a pleasant town, designed in the traditional fashion, with the county courthouse in the center of a square flanked by stores. He passed three churches, two banks, and a library. Most of the people lived west of the square, in small ranch houses with carports, similar to his sister's house. He made two turns and slowed half a block from Peggy's address. Her mailbox was visible, bright and shiny in the sun. He considered slipping the envelope in the box and leaving, but he wanted to see her one more time. If nothing else, she should have a chance to see him, in case he didn't make it back from the Mushroom Mines. It wasn't selfish, he told himself. He was thinking of her.

He drove forward and stopped in front of a house built of brick with white shutters and aluminum window frames. Peggy's car was in the driveway. A wrought iron rail led to a low concrete stoop. The gutters were clean, the downspout gleaming. He left the truck, took a breath, walked across the grass, and knocked on the door. Nobody answered, but he could hear a television inside. He knocked again, louder. She was probably taking a walk, he thought, maybe pushing a stroller. There was no sidewalk, and he hoped she was being careful of traffic. He knocked a third time. Again, no answer, which gave him a surprising sense of relief. He went to the mailbox, then wondered if it was better to put the letter inside the screen door. She might have already gathered the mail. But maybe they didn't use the front door, entering instead through the side door off the carport. He stood immobile and unsure.

"Mick?"

He turned and saw her coming around the side of the house holding a one-year-old on her hip. The baby's hair was the same color as her mother's. Peggy wore cutoff jeans and a light blue sleeveless blouse. Her forearms were freshly freckled, as if she spent more time in the sun now.

"I knocked," he said.

"I was around back with Ruby."

"She looks like you."

"You think so?"

"Yes," he said. "You look good."

"I don't know," she said. "I've still got the baby weight on me."

Mick nodded. He was uncertain as to her meaning. The baby looked as if she weighed about twenty pounds, not so much weight. He didn't know how to continue the conversation. There was very little sound on the street. A wind chime rang like a distant church bell. Somewhere a screen door banged shut. All the houses looked the same.

"Nice place," he said.

"I like it. How's your leg?"

"Feels okay."

Ruby squirmed, and Peggy squatted to place the child on the ground. She wore a long yellow shirt over a diaper. Squinting her tiny brown eyes against the sun, she held her mother's leg.

"Well," Peggy said.

"I signed the papers."

Peggy blinked twice, then smiled in a way Mick hadn't seen in many years. He'd made her happy, he realized, which pleased him. The method of providing it wrenched him.

"Thank you," she said.

"I have to go," he said. "Heading back to base soon."

"Say hi to Linda."

He nodded and got in the truck. She'd already turned away, moving slowly, her attention on Ruby. He turned around in the neighbor's driveway. By the time he passed Peggy's house she was gone. He went back through town, took Slate Avenue to the interstate, and drove to Rocksalt.

It pained him that her life was better than when they'd lived together. He felt an immeasurable sorrow.

At Linda's house he wrote a will, signed and dated the paper, and tucked it into his suitcase. He went to bed early and lay there wishing he had Percocet or whiskey or both.

Chapter Twenty

Linda snapped awake, her body already tense with anxiety about the day's election. She didn't need coffee but drank it anyhow to prevent a midday headache from withdrawal. She brushed her hair and tucked it into a bun behind her head, then dressed in her newest uniform, fresh from the dry cleaner. In the mirror she considered applying makeup. It was possible she'd appear in a photograph or on a social media video. A little makeup wouldn't hurt. She hadn't worn any since her last date and had overdone it then. Okay, Linda, she said to herself. Stop it. Go to work.

She put on her duty belt, carried her hat to the kitchen, and rinsed the coffee cup. Her brother was still in bed, and she moved quietly. Lately he'd been more distant than usual. In the car she slid the official sheriff's hat over her head, adjusted it in the rearview mirror, and drove to the station. The night dispatcher shook her head to indicate no calls were pending. She appeared sleepy. Her husband worked for the electric company, which kept him away from the house at all hours.

"Go on home," Linda said.

"You sure? It's early."

"Yeah, go get your kids ready for school. I'll stay till Sandra comes on shift."

"Thank you," the dispatcher said. "Little Pete's in first grade now, and I ain't seen Big Pete in four days. That big storm knocked out power in three counties. He's traipsing the woods hunting the break."

Linda went into her office and looked at the day's schedule. Yet another pancake breakfast in an hour. Then a quick stop at an elderly care center, timed before the residents boarded the bus for the polls. Lunch and a speech to the Young Democrats club at the college. If kids and old folks voted for her, she'd be all right—as long as the weather held. After lunch were two more stops, both involving food, then a final event at what she hoped would be a victory celebration. Polls closed at six o'clock.

She ran through notes for her stump speeches, updating a couple and making changes. Every time she spoke in public, her opponent had someone taking notes, then he'd deliver a variation. It was flattering that she was worth copying, but each speech required new elements. A few days ago she'd omitted any mention of the hostage situation at the Dollar General, because no one was hurt and everyone liked Jaybird Watts. He was in an alcohol program, with the promise of his old job back upon completion. She added a short anecdote about the need for social services instead of jail time for first offenders on a drug charge. Families appreciated that.

The front door opened and closed. She recognized Johnny Boy's tread before he stuck his head in the office.

"Morning," he said. "Ready for the big day? Bet you didn't sleep a wink."

"Slept like a baby. Cried all night and shit the bed."

Johnny Boy frowned and withdrew to his own office. She knew he'd never cared for the rough language. Nobody really did except Mick, who thought it was funny. His leg was clearly better, which meant he'd be going back to Germany soon. She checked the clock on her phone. It was time to go. She went to Johnny Boy's office, where he was intent on organizing his extensive files.

"Got to roll," she said. "Stay here until Sandra comes, then take care of any calls. If there aren't any, you can drive around and make sure nobody's kicking my signs over."

"Yes, ma'am."

"I'll see you at the community center at five."

"Which one?"

"On the bypass."

"Which one?"

"Which one what, Johnny Boy?"

"Bypass. There's two."

"There's only one community center on a bypass."

"Yep," he said, "on Flemingsburg Road. The Carl D. Perkins Community Center. The 'D.' stands for Dewey.

You know he had a lisp? Said it helped make him a man of the people. Maybe you should add a lisp to your speeches."

"Shut the fuck up, Johnny Boy."

She left and waved to Sandra, who was getting out of her car in the parking lot.

"Good luck, Sheriff," Sandra said.

"Do you think I'm a woman of the people?"

"Yes, for women especially. Older men, maybe not. The young people don't care that much about gender anymore. It's all fluid, you know, in flux."

"What are you talking about?"

"Nothing," Sandra said. "You got my vote and my family's."

"Thank you. I look all right?"

"Great. You look great."

Linda nodded and drove to the American Legion to try and not eat too many pancakes. She'd never liked them.

Chapter Twenty-One

Raymond was a vegetarian, which made him a pariah in Appalachia. For breakfast he prepared an omelet with cheese, onion, ramps, and a diced turnip. His mother refused to take a bite and demanded sausage and eggs with light-bread toast. He did as he was told, and she ate silently, then retreated to the porch to smoke cigarettes and drink coffee. He wasn't worried about her. In the Corps he'd learned that fretting never got anyone anywhere. There were always two options—fight or comply. He preferred compliance in general, particularly with senior officers, his mother, or Juan Carlos, waiting for him in San Diego. Juan Carlos had already texted him twice this morning.

Raymond washed the dishes and sent J.C. a text that all was fine. In a broom closet he found a stack of paper bags from the IGA, which he laid over the table. He carried the weapons to the kitchen—a Glock 9mm, a SIG Sauer M17 pistol, and two Colt M4 submachine guns. He disassembled each gun, cleaned it thoroughly, and put it back together. The familiar scent of solvent and oil filled the kitchen. The weapons gleamed in the dull light. He went out the front door, where his mother stared at the tree line along the road.

"Mommy," he said.

After several seconds she slowly turned her head to look at him. A relative had given her some lorazepam, and he wondered how many she'd taken.

"Mommy," he said, "I'm going to do some shooting out back. Target practice."

She returned her gaze to the trees. A pair of starlings flew in a low arc across the yard a few feet from the porch. She didn't react. Raymond went into the house, gathered the guns, and left through the back door. He set them on an old picnic table he'd eaten at as a child. From the IGA bags he fashioned crude targets and placed them at intervals up the hill to the woods. The M4 had a maximum efficiency of six hundred feet, but due to his combat experience, Raymond felt more comfortable at close quarters. He set the trigger at single fire, then three-round bursts and full auto, pleased with the accuracy of both rifles. The pistols were satisfactory as well. He sighted in the SIG Sauer for himself, then went inside. His phone had two more messages from Juan Carlos and a text from Hardin saying he was on his way over.

Raymond checked on his mother, who hadn't moved. He made her a cup of coffee and himself some tea. They sat quietly, looking at nothing. Gradually a few birds called, as if testing the air, having been silenced by the gunfire. Raymond sent Juan Carlos a text with a string of emojis. He thought that style of communication was silly, but J.C. enjoyed the tiny images.

"Son," Shifty said without moving.

"Mom."

"That didn't sound like a rifle or shotgun back there."

"It wasn't."

"This have to do with your brothers?"

"Yes."

"Good," she said. "You'll be careful."

"I will."

The sun had risen far enough above the hill to cross the road and reach the porch. Shifty slid the house shoes off and wiggled her toes in the heat. He recalled her doing that when he was a child. It occurred to Raymond that he might not survive the night.

"Mommy," he said.

"Son."

"Something I need to tell you."

She waited silently.

"I'm gay," he said.

"I know it."

"You do?"

"I always did," she said.

"You never said anything."

"I didn't know how."

Raymond considered this. It seemed far-fetched that his deepest secret had been known to her for years. His sense of his own past seemed to shift within him.

"I don't have a Mexican girlfriend," he said.

"Reckon not," she said.

"It's a man."

"A wife-husband?"

"We're not married."

The sun rose along her legs, and she gently pulled her housecoat up to reveal her shins. The skin was dry.

"You want some lotion for your legs?" he said.

"No, thank you. Your uncle was that way, too. It's in the family."

"Dry legs?"

She squeezed out a tiny laugh. As the oldest of five, his job as a child had been twofold—her little helper and entertainer. They were at their best when he did both.

"Which one?" he said.

"Uncle Henry."

"I never met him."

"Your daddy's brother. He got killed for it when he was sixteen. Nobody talked about it back then. Your daddy, he was on the lookout for it in all of y'all. That's why he raised you boys hard."

"Thought he could beat it out of us?"

"No, son," she said. "So you could fight back if a one of you was that way. Your daddy didn't want to lose a boy like he lost his brother."

Raymond's tea was cold, but he drank it anyway. He'd felt desires for men since he was twelve, understood it fully at sixteen, but never acted on it until after boot camp at Pendleton. He'd rented a car and driven to LA and found a bar in West Hollywood. A wild and contradictory thought crossed his mind. He was glad his father died young and didn't have to mourn the deaths of three sons, but Raymond wished he was still alive to see the gay one fighting for the family.

He heard an engine and watched the road. Mick's pickup truck rolled into view, slowing for the turn. He parked on the grass, which was still packed down from all the vehicles after the funeral. For the sake of decorum, Shifty pushed the housecoat in place over her bare legs.

"Hidy, Mrs. Kissick," Mick said.

She tipped her chin in a silent greeting and resumed her surveillance of the woods. Mick followed Raymond to the back of the house. The arms lay in a row on the picnic table. Beside them were sixteen spare clips, four per weapon.

"You run rounds through them?" Mick said.

"Yeah. They're in better shape than I expected. I sighted in the M4s and the SIG."

Mick nodded. He picked up the Glock, checked the chamber, and slid a clip in place. He took a two-handed isosceles stance and fired twice at the closest target, twice at one midrange, and twice at the farthest. He walked across the field, still dewy enough to wet his boots but not his pants legs. He'd hit all three targets close to center but slightly high and to the right. After adjusting the sights, he fired at each target again, satisfied with the results. The M4 had a one-point sling that was too long, and he tightened it to suit his right arm. On full auto he fired at the first target and watched pieces of paper tatter the air. He switched the lever to three-burst, lowered the sling, then lifted it rapidly and shot the second target. He unfolded the collapsible stock, aimed carefully at the last target high on the hill, and fired.

"You hit it," Raymond said. "Not bad."

He lowered a monocular from his eye.

"The Langes give us that?" Mick said.

"Naw, it was laying around the house. Mason used to hunt deer. A month before the season opened, he'd leave clothes and equipment in the deer stand. Said the deer would get used to the smell."

"If a deer's close enough to smell clothes, they'd smell him."

"I told him that," Raymond said. "Didn't do no good."

"Did Barney hunt?"

"No. Didn't hunt, fish, or fight. Never knew him to finish a chore. Mason kept things going as far as I can tell. Barney, he was a case."

"Must've been good at something."

"Math. Good head for business. Women liked him. Never had a regular girlfriend but moved around. You know, one here, one there. Mommy might have grand-babies all over the county."

"Uncle Ray-Ray."

Mick walked across the backyard and up the hill, gathering the targets. Raymond picked up the shell casings. They sat at the picnic table and cleaned the weapons. A squirrel watched them from a hickory tree. Mick nodded to it in a friendly way, knowing he might die later and never see another squirrel.

"I got divorced yesterday," Mick said.

"I came out to my mom."

They looked at the woods. The squirrel was gone. Mick stood and spoke.

"I'll come get you at sixteen-thirty."

Mick left. Raymond carried the weapons back to the kitchen. He made another cup of coffee for his mother, and they sat in silence on the porch. Raymond wondered what his mother was thinking about but preferred not to ask. He looked at his mother's profile, shoulders back, her expression as steady as a granite cliff against a storm. He studied her profile, trying to memorize it in case he got shot at the mines. He'd fit her image into his mind as he died.

Chapter Twenty-Two

On the way to town, Mick passed a small limestone voting house with a line of people waiting to enter. Campaign posters swayed like weeds along the road. Mick parked in the sheriff department's lot beside Sandra's car and crossed the faded gray asphalt. The two spots reserved for the sheriff and deputy were vacant. Inside, Sandra sat at her desk, phone receiver cradled to her ear, writing on a pad. She nodded, said thank you, hung up the phone, and regarded Mick.

"Hello, Deputy," she said. "Got a call for you. A woman saw a coyote by her chicken coop."

"Is that a crime?"

"Yes, it is. We have a special coyote jail out back."

Mick nodded.

"I'm kidding," she said.

"I'm not a deputy anymore. I resigned."

"If we're not officially working together, let's have lunch."

"Uh, I don't know about that."

"You'll have to run get it," she said. "Linda is campaigning, and she's got Johnny Boy going to precincts until a call comes in. It's just me all day."

Mick nodded.

"There's Mexican," she said. "Chinese. Italian. Plus all the usual fast-food places."

"What do you like?"

She shrugged, a sheepish expression on her face.

"Dairy Queen," she said.

"You order, and I'll get it. Bacon cheeseburger with raw onion, small fries, water with no ice."

He drove to Dairy Queen, waited five minutes for the food, and returned to the sheriff's department. Sandra had cleared off a corner of her desk and moved a chair so they could sit at an angle to each other. She'd ordered a combo plate with fries and a blue slushy. He waited for her to take the first bite. She did so with a gusto that he had seen only in Italy, the pure joy of eating for the sake of flavor and smell.

Sandra licked her fingers, wiped her mouth, and sat back.

"You're lost in thought," she said. "Something going on?"

"Not really."

"Is it me?"

He shook his head, hoping she'd let it go. She might take his explanation as an evaluation of her eating style. He needed to change the subject.

"I dropped off my divorce papers," he said.

"This just gets more romantic."

"I'm not legally divorced but almost."

"Is this your idea of a booty call?"

"No," he said. "I don't know what it is. Lunch. I thought . . . I mean. I don't know what I mean. It's not that."

"I'm kidding, Mick. Did anyone ever tell you that you're too serious?"

He nodded.

"You know any jokes?" she said.

"Just one," he said. "A termite walks into a tavern and says, 'Is the bar tender here?'"

He watched her frown as she sorted through the joke, repeating it mentally to herself. She gave him a quick glance to ascertain if there was more. Then she leaned back, tilted her face toward the ceiling, and laughed as if she'd been saving up for a month.

"Good one," she said. "Best I've heard in a while."

"It's easy to remember."

"I'll tell Uncle Robin. He likes any jokes about animals."

"Is a termite an animal?"

"Yes, it's not a plant or a fungi, bacteria or a protist."

"How do you come to know that?"

"I paid attention in science class."

Mick nodded. Maybe town schools were better than out in the county, or maybe he'd missed that week. He'd often been absent to help his grandfather with outdoor tasks. The school didn't mind because he was a solid A student, a result of reading the textbooks the first week of classes, then reading them again each night before a test.

"You're thinking in your head again," she said.

"Yeah. About school. It was too easy."

"College, too?"

"The easiest. I didn't take much science."

"What did you study?"

"Criminology. Minor in psychology. Took a while because I was on active duty, but the army paid for it. You?"

"Poli-sci for two years at Rocksalt. Transferred to UK for pre-law."

"No law school?"

"I didn't really like it. Too much lying and playing angles. Then I got married and came back here, and that didn't work out. Day I signed my divorce papers was the happiest day in years. What about you?"

"More like relieved, I guess. We were miserable a long time and didn't know it. Then it got pretty messy. Being happy hasn't figured in yet. It was never a goal. I always saw happiness as a by-product."

"Of what?"

"Of living right. Making the right decision."

"Are my teeth blue?" she said.

"A little, from that slushy."

"Good."

"You want that?" he said.

"Makes me look fearsome if somebody gets brought in."

He nodded, a half smile drifting across his face.

"When is your leave up?" she said.

"Two days."

"Dang," she said. "That's perfect."

Mick nodded. He didn't know what she meant. A long, quiet minute passed between them.

"I've got tomorrow off," she said.

"A Wednesday?"

"I've been putting in a lot of time covering here. Johnny Boy's on tomorrow. Your sister will either celebrate winning the election or be down in the dumps."

"With her, either one's as bad as the other."

She laughed again. Mick wadded the scraps of their food in the burger wrappers and stood.

"I'll put this outside so it won't smell your office up," he said.

"Come over to my house for supper."

"Can't," he said. "Something I've got to do."

"Later, then," she said. "We can have a beer and listen to the cicadas."

"It might run real late."

"Are you brushing me off?"

"No," he said. "I don't know when I'll be done."

"When men talk that way it means a woman or a poker game."

"Neither."

"If the porch light's on," she said, "I'm up."

He nodded and left. The noon sun glared off the parking lot and made deep shadows in the shrubbery. He threw the food wrappers in a garbage can, wondering what had just transpired. He drove to his sister's house, undressed, and lay in bed. Usually he was a champion napper, a skill necessary to soldiers, but his mind spun circles around lunch. He couldn't remember having talked so much and didn't understand why he had.

At three o'clock, he dressed in dark clothing and found a first aid kit in a kitchen drawer. It was from a drugstore, good for minor cuts and little else. He removed a tube of antibiotic ointment and four large adhesive bandages. He slid them in a cargo pocket along with a roll of duct tape, a pair of pliers, superglue, a flashlight, and a portable sewing kit. It wasn't much but would have to do. From a shed attached to the carport he took a pair of work gloves and a shovel, knowing he might have to dig for the suitcase. He stowed everything in the truck, drove to the Kissick home place, and parked on the grass.

Raymond came outside wearing a lightweight tactical chest rig with spare clips, a canteen, and the SIG Sauer holstered across his chest. On his head was a black ball cap with no insignia. He gave Mick a chest harness, the Glock, and a communications headset. In the backyard they tested the comm sets at five hundred and a thousand yards with good results. Mick drove silently along single-lane blacktop roads to Lawton. He pointed to the turnoff for the Mushroom Mines and went past it to a dirt lane that curved out of sight and ended at a grassy field. He parked the truck and cut the engine.

"It's a mile up that road," Mick said. "One way in and out. Best to leave the vehicle here."

"You do much roving recon?" Raymond said.

"Before CID, yeah. Been a while. You?"

"It's one of my specialties."

Mick nodded, and Raymond got out of the truck.

"You get jammed up," Mick said, "give me a Mayday and go to the road. I'll be there."

Raymond stepped into the woods, moving low and quiet. If he had to flee on foot, Mick wanted to make it easier for exfil. He practiced leaning across the bench seat and opening the passenger door six times, then closed his eyes and did it six more times. He relaxed his body as much as possible. The seat was lumpy and sprung, covered with foam padding leaking from the seams. The rule of thumb for soldiers was to eat and sleep when you could, because it might be days before you got another chance. The rest of the time you waited—waited for orders, waited for chow, waited in formation. The worst was waiting in an aircraft for your turn to jump.

He breathed slowly and performed simple math in his head, keeping his vision moving along the tree line. As the sun dipped behind the hill, twilight seemed to rise from the earth. The gray air between the trees turned dark. A few lightning bugs appeared low to the ground, females attracting males with their luminescence. Frogs sounded like the rasping of machinery rusted by weather. A barred owl called, then another, both declaring territory. A female began her high-pitched rising squawk, and the males answered. The lightning bugs proliferated, hundreds of winking specks in the field beyond the truck. A bat shot past the windshield, veering wildly as it snatched insects from the air.

Mick checked the time—a mere ten minutes had passed. It felt like much longer, and he returned to his calculated breathing. He couldn't allow his mind to drift to Sandra, the election, his ex-wife and her baby, the charred ruins of the cabin built by his great-grandfather. Trying not to drift was its own form of drift. He'd suppressed his anger until it hollowed him like the shell of a box turtle found in the woods—a hard exterior that surrounded empty space. Nothing mattered but staying alive. He didn't care about anything or anyone. He didn't care about Raymond, only extracting him to safety.

Adrenaline was poised in his body, ready to surge. Beginning with his toes, he tightened and relaxed his muscles, mentally moving up each leg, then starting fresh with his fingers and arms. He rolled his shoulders and neck, hearing the slight pop of tendons. The lightning bugs vanished. Night had fully arrived. The strip of sky between the hills filled with garlands of stars.

He recalled his grandfather teaching him how to walk silently at night in the woods—place the outer edge of each boot on the ground, then slowly settle the sole. At the first faint resistance or rustle of a twig, you stopped and moved your other foot forward. He'd practiced for weeks, until it was instinctive and he was able to sneak up on his grandfather from behind. After that, Papaw began instructions in how to negotiate darkness. He made two patties of dough, pressed them against Mick's eye sockets, wrapped a strip of cloth twice around his head, and tied it off. He told Mick to stay in one place for three hours at the edge of the yard. It was a lesson in listening as well as accepting the inability to see. The next day Mick walked ten feet into the woods, his arms held in the recommended position—one at a diagonal in front of his face, the other at a right angle before his torso—in order to protect himself from low limbs and briars. Each day he walked farther, for a longer period, scratching his face and arms. Oh, that's a scrape, he'd think, then isolate the sensation and ignore it. Eventually pain mattered as little as sight.

After a month of lessons, Papaw removed the blindfold. The key to seeing at night, he explained, was to not look directly at anything. If Mick kept his vision moving, flicking his focus about, he could maximize his peripheral abilities. In average darkness he could see fifteen or so feet in front, to each side, and behind him. As he walked, this limitation moved with him, encasing him until it ceased to be a constraint.

An hour and a half passed. A few insects entered the open windows of the truck cab. He brushed them casually away without sound. The frogs had ceased their racket. Mick figured thirty minutes for Raymond to get up the hill, an hour and a half of recon, and another thirty minutes for return. Plus or minus an hour. Despite not knowing Raymond well, Mick trusted his training. One Marine from Trinity was plenty against a small force.

He heard a slight rustle outside the truck and leaned back to reduce his silhouette. His comm set clicked twice. "I'm here," Raymond said.

A minute later Raymond opened the passenger door and climbed in, ignoring the pistol. He drank from his canteen and wiped his mouth. Tipping his head back, he spoke to the bare metal ceiling of the cab.

"Nine hostiles," he said. "One on the hill above the entrance. He's got a sniper rifle with a tripod and thermal imaging sights. No spotter, he's on his own. Two fixed sentries on the perimeter, one on either side of the road, east and west. Five more patrolling the entrance. There's four tents, unoccupied. Three vehicles. One's a camper van for mess."

"Arms?"

"AR-15s with spare clips. No sidearms on the ones outside."

"Assessment?"

"Hardened operators. The sentries have comms."

Mick nodded, staring at the darkened tree line.

"Evaluation?" he said.

"Contradictory. They're set up to keep people out, not repel an assault. But the force is bigger than they need. The sniper is confusing. He has a long-range rifle, but the kill zone is small. Unnecessary and impractical."

"Maybe that's his training. They're using what they got."

"He'll need to be neutralized first."

"Options?"

"We attack now. Or we wait."

"Let's give them time to get bored and tired."

Mick started the truck and followed 174 through the hills to Open Fork. Several years ago his old grade school had burned mysteriously, leaving the limestone shell with no roof. Mick drove behind the school and parked beside the old boiler room. His favorite memory of school was sitting in the boiler room on cold mornings talking to the janitor, Mr. Tucker. A shallow creek ran beside the school. During periods of drought, Mr. Tucker carried buckets of water down the creek bank to replenish the isolated pools and keep the minnows alive.

"Rest time," Raymond said. "You want the back?"

"You're bigger. You take it."

Raymond left the cab and climbed into the truck bed, the leaf shocks shifting from the weight. Mick set his phone alarm. He shifted across the bench seat and lay on his back with his knees bent. He considered opening the door for his legs, but they'd hang out and put strain on his lower back. If he propped his boots in the open window, his knees would stiffen up. He'd slept on worse—strapped into a troop transport aircraft, on a concrete floor in a makeshift bivouac, for two weeks on solid rock in Syria. He imagined lying on a beach beneath a cerulean sky with a horizon line the same color as the sea. He could hear the surf approach and recede in tandem with his breath. He was warm and calm. He slept.

Chapter Twenty-Three

The phone alarm woke Mick two hours later. Through the windshield he saw Raymond performing tai chi in the moonlight. The clear sky blazed with stars. Mick got out of the truck and stretched the stiffness from his back and limbs. He and Raymond discussed the mission, settling on a flexible plan and comm codes.

They drove back to the Mushroom Mines and parked at the foot of the hill. Mick tucked the Beretta in the glove box and holstered the Glock. They carried the M4s through the woods and began climbing the hill parallel to the road. The night was quiet, the sky clear, a half-moon suspended like a broken plate.

Near the top Raymond stopped walking and spoke in a whisper.

"What's the R.O.E.?"

Mick lifted his face to meet Raymond's eyes. Asking the rules of engagement was the sign of a solid Marine.

"This isn't a war," Mick said. "Eliminate all threat. Save one for interrogation."

Raymond vanished into the darkness, and Mick moved east to a rain gully. He double-checked the M4, then began a slow, silent climb toward the sentry posted at the top of the road. He crawled a few feet, stopped to listen for a minute, and resumed progress. Sweat dampened his clothes. Twice he saw the eyes of nocturnal scavengers and halted until they moved on. Above him, silhouetted against the sky, was a set of human shoulders and a head. Mick shifted for a better view and realized the sentry was leaning against an oak. Mick lifted the M4, breathing through his mouth to reduce any sound. The man was alert but not wary, watching the road instead of the hill.

Mick cleared his mind and imagined a burning rock, an old battle trick. I'm the rock, he thought. I'm the fire. Nothing can hurt me. He kept the gun sights trained on the man's head. He ignored the insects that found him. I'm the burning rock. His comm set clicked twice, meaning the sniper was down. Mick continued to wait. The sentry rolled his shoulders and shifted his weight, then marched briefly in place, oblivious to Mick's surveillance. Half an hour passed. The sentry walked in a circle, then returned to his spot beside the oak.

Mick relaxed his muscles to prevent stiffness. Once the action began, he'd need full mobility. I am the rock, I am the fire. Nothing can hurt me. His comm clicked three times. Raymond was in position for the other sentry. Mick tightened his grip and realigned the sights on the target. He tipped the toes of his boots for traction. He spoke in the lightest of whispers.

"One. Two. Three. Go."

He squeezed the trigger, and the sentry fell. The sound of his weapon was loud in his ears, but he could hear the echo of Raymond's shot. Mick sprang forward, switching the mode of fire to a three-round burst. Tree branches scraped his face and arms. He charged across the road to the unfinished structures, looking for the foot patrol. He crouched in the blocky shadow of a wall. From his left came the sound of an AR-15 on full auto. Raymond had engaged.

Mick moved to the edge of the wall. Leading with the barrel of his rifle, he poked his head around the corner and jerked it back to draw fire. Bullets struck the wall where his head had been. One round passed through the wall, showering him with chips of concrete. He ran to the other end of the wall, rounded the corner, saw the enemy, and fired a burst. The man fell into the darkness. Mick charged forward. The man lay on his back, swinging an AR-15 one-handed into firing position. He got off a wild burst before Mick shot him in the chest.

Mick kept moving. He heard footsteps to his right and shifted direction mid-stride, firing at the sound, then leaped to cover behind a low brick structure. Capped water pipes protruded from the top. He was exposed on three sides. The enemy could pick him off easily.

With a sudden motion, he ran across the field toward the farthest building, firing on full auto to suppress the enemy. The M4 jammed. He slammed into the brick wall, dropped the rifle, and withdrew the Glock. Behind him was the sporadic noise of Raymond's firefight. Mick waited. He heard the soft scuff of boots on loose rock. The man came around the corner of the building, and Mick shot him twice. He holstered his pistol, scooped up the enemy's AR-15, and ran toward Raymond.

He came upon a more fully built structure—three walls, a doorway, and two openings for windows. No floor or roof. A man was shooting from inside. Mick peered around the edge of the doorway. The man spun, fired a burst, then jumped out the low opening of the window. Mick pivoted to sidle along the exterior wall. It was in deep shadow but utterly exposed to the open field where the enemy had fled. There was no sound. He saw motion behind a low mound of hardened cement and fired. Both shots ricocheted off the cement and a man ran at a diagonal, heading for the tree line. Mick shot twice more. The man continued running. Automatic fire came from Mick's left and the man staggered with momentum then fell. In a running crouch, Mick approached the bloodstained weeds and shot the man twice.

A minute of silence passed. Mick spoke into his comm set.

"Sit-rep," he said.

"Four down. One prisoner."

"What's your twenty?"

"Woods on your side of the road."

"Coming to you."

Mick moved in a combat stance across the land, abruptly pivoting to check behind him every few steps. If their math was correct, they'd eliminated all threat, but Raymond could have missed a man on recon. The field began to slope toward the tree line, and Raymond rose from the brush. Mick lowered his gun and switched on his flashlight. Two men lay on the ground, one dead, one wounded. The front of Raymond's shirt was dark with blood. Mick gestured to the wet stain.

"You hit?"

"A through-and-through. Nothing vital."

"Let me take a look."

"After we interrogate this asshole," Raymond said.

He pointed at the prone man, who had been shot twice in the right leg and once in the hand. His eyes were open. He was losing blood but not too fast. His hand was a wreck of splintered bone and cartilage.

"He say anything?" Mick said.

"Nothing."

Mick squatted and put a flashlight in the man's eyes. He blinked rapidly. His pupils were dilated.

"Might be concussed," Mick said.

"No doubt. I clubbed him."

"After you shot him?"

"He gave my position away. Keeping him alive got me tagged."

Raymond prodded the man, who moaned. Mick aimed his weapon across the field in case anyone else showed up. The night was quiet. A slight breeze brushed the broad leaves of poplar. The half-moon cast long shadows from the abandoned structures. An owl called twice, as if the carnage had never occurred.

Raymond dragged the man to a sitting position against a tree and doused his face with canteen water. The man spluttered.

"What's your name?" Raymond said.

"Kowalski."

"You're in bad shape. You need medical assistance. Answer some questions, and I'll help you. Understand?"

The man nodded, grimacing.

"How many men here?" Raymond said.

"Nine."

"You lying?"

"No."

Raymond glanced at Mick, who nodded. They'd removed all the enemy. Mick lowered his weapon and squatted beside Kowalski.

"The trucks that come up here," Mick said. "What's in them?"

"I don't know."

Raymond pressed the barrel of his gun against the wound on the man's leg.

"Talk, asshole."

"I don't know," Kowalski said. "It's long sacks. Hazardous waste, the drivers think. They haul the sacks way deep in the mine. Drive right in there."

"How far back?"

"Pretty far. Sergeant Russo knows more."

"Which one's he?"

"Older. Gray-headed. He's got some sort of ring on. Turns color if it gets hot."

"A dosimeter ring?" Mick said. "For radiation."

The man nodded wildly, pulling his leg away from Raymond.

"Yeah, yeah," he said. "The sergeant, he's got it and a wristband."

"Okay," Mick said. "You're doing good."

The man stared at Mick with a hopeful expression despite his pain.

"How long you worked here?" Mick said.

"A month."

"Good. Only a couple more questions, all right?"

The man nodded rapidly, flicking his vision to Raymond as if to confirm.

"Look at me," Mick said. "Not him."

The man complied. Raymond scared him, which Mick wanted and would exploit. He forced his voice to a conversational tone.

"Last week," he said. "Not sure which day. A man came up here name of Barney. Remember that?"

"Yeah."

"Did you kill him?"

"No."

"Who did?"

"Sergeant Russo."

"Where's Barney's vehicle?"

"He paid a driver to haul it off."

"Another man came a few days later. What happened to him?"

"Ricky found him. The sergeant shot him, then sent Ricky and Preston to town with the car and the body. I don't know what they did."

"Okay," Mick said. "You're doing good. Almost there. My buddy here's ready for triage. He's a medic."

"Yep," Raymond said. "I'll fix you up."

Raymond shifted his weight and patted his pocket as if proving he had first aid material. The man nodded.

"Who burnt the cabin down?" Mick said.

"Uh . . . ," Kowalksi said. "What cabin?"

"You know what cabin."

"It was empty. Sarge said to burn it."

"Did you do it?"

The man didn't speak. Raymond stepped on his wounded hand.

"I didn't light it," the man said. "It wasn't me!"

Raymond pivoted his boot. The man screamed and passed out.

"Shit," Raymond said.

"Let me see your wound," Mick said.

Raymond lifted his shirt. The bullet had gone in from the front and exited, missing the hip bone and vital organs. Mick cleaned the entrance wound with water, then smeared the topical antibiotic salve on a large bandage. He applied the bandage and cleaned the exit hole. The wound was clean, not jagged, and bleeding steadily.

"It needs stitches," Mick said. "You want the hospital?"

"No fucking way."

Mick removed the tube of superglue from his pocket.

"Fucking army medic," Raymond said.

Mick dried the wound as best he could, ran a line of glue along the exposed flesh and skin, then pinched the wound together. He released his fingers, and the hole was closed. He waited thirty seconds, applied a bandage, and wrapped a length of duct tape around Raymond's torso.

"Glue will peel off in a few days," Mick said.

"What about him?"

They looked at Kowalski, who had begun to stir.

"He needs a doctor," Mick said.

"He can ID us."

"Nobody will believe him. I'll be in Europe, and you'll be in California."

"Mommy wants me to stay."

"You going to?"

"For a while."

"I'll get the transport."

Mick walked down the dirt road. After combat he preferred to be alone, to walk off the vestiges of adrenaline and intense fear. The last time had been several years ago in Afghanistan, an operation based on flawed intelligence that resulted in sixteen dead American troops. Mick was wounded twice but continued fighting and later received a Silver Star for valor. He recovered and joined the CID. Killing during war was lawful, but nothing about the current mission was legal. He'd murdered the sentry, then killed civilians defending themselves. He'd done the very thing he'd struggled against his entire life—killed for vengeance. As much as he'd tried to get away, he was still bound by the hills. He didn't like killing, he was just good at it. He could justify his actions, the same as every man he'd taken into custody. Briefly he hated himself, then pushed it aside. His feelings didn't matter, had never been important.

At the foot of the hill he drank half his canteen, wondering if he was burned out. Maybe it was PTSD. His bad leg ached from exertion. A new possibility assailed him—he was angry about the divorce and flinging his rage at strangers. He examined the idea and discarded it. Divorce made him sad, but the source of his fury was Jacky. He'd died because the men at the mines thought he was Mick lying in bed. It was cowardice on their part. Taking money to kill was their decision. They lived by the sword. Now they lay in their own blood. One day Mick would, too.

He cut through the woods to the truck. He drove with his headlights on dim, barely illuminating the road. At the top he turned around and parked in the dark shadows of the tree line. Retrieving the shovel from the bed, he crossed the field to Raymond, who met him at the top of the weedy slope.

"Where's the prisoner?" Mick said.

"He didn't make it."

"We needed him to find out who's behind the dumping."

"They work for Blacksword Security out of Texas. All ex-military. The sergeant talks by cell phone to someone at Buckner Disposal. He heard calls to someone he thought was a boss. Mr. Knox."

"Murvil Knox?"

"No first name. He told them to put heroin on Fuckin' Barney. Something about a yellow crown."

"Where'd they get it?"

"Knox's man."

Mick turned away, preferring not to know how Raymond learned the information. He headed to the mine opening.

"I'll go in," Mick said. "Your mom thinks he hid it close to the entrance."

"Yeah, well, she thinks the moon landing was a hoax."

"Uncle Robin worked here fifty years ago. He said there was an office inside."

Mick clipped the flashlight to his chest rig and turned it on. He slid his hands into the leather work gloves and carried the shovel into the dark opening on the side of the hill. The flashlight's beam barely pierced the blackness. The floor was a mess of footprints and tire tracks that continued into the dark interior. On Mick's right was a small room adorned with spray-painted graffiti. A few rotting timbers lay against the wall. Overhead was the remnant of a light socket, the copper wiring stolen long ago. The only sound was a faint dripping deep within the earth. It was a good place for snakes, but he figured the passage of men and trucks had driven them out. He turned in a circle, looking for evidence of soft earth, a place where Barney had buried his aunt's suitcase. Nothing. The walls were solid stone, which meant going deeper into the bowels of the earth.

He walked slowly along one wall, examining the limestone for disturbed dirt. In the dim beam of the flashlight everything looked uniform. The black air was cool and humid. He came to a room with a thirty-foot ceiling and two passages, left and right, that ended in utter darkness. He could hear his own breathing and nothing else. Behind him, the entrance was a small square of light. He had an impulse to rush toward it, to flee the enveloping darkness. Several deep breaths calmed him, and he decided that Barney wouldn't have continued. The walls were stone, with nowhere to hide a parcel. It would be closer to the entrance, probably buried.

Mick walked back the way he'd come, carefully inspecting the other wall. It was solid. The dirt below appeared undisturbed. He wondered if he'd been wrong, if the enemy had found the suitcase. The silhouette of Raymond stood at the entrance facing out, weapon at the ready. Mick was more relieved than he expected.

He used the shovel to gouge the packed dirt, working in parallel lines across the first room as if aerating soil. The blade struck rock a few inches below the surface. He finished the grid search disappointed and went to a decaying stack of racks that had once held hundreds of mushrooms. With the shovel as a fulcrum, he strained to shift the rack a few inches from the wall. He went from side to side, shoving the rack until he could see the dirt beneath it. Again the blade hit rock. Nothing was buried under the rack. The wall behind it was discolored in a low arch rising from the floor. He pressed the shovel into soft earth that filled the arch. He had to move the rack two more feet to gain access. Despite the cool air, he was sweating heavily. He scraped dirt from an opening that he realized was part of the ventilation system put in place by the mushroom farmers. The clay dirt was packed in tight, then very loosely. The blade struck something pliable. He shoveled small loads of dirt, revealing a square case with a handle. Mick carried it to the entrance and stepped out, grateful for the clear air, the plume of stars to the east, and a breeze that cooled his face.

"Time to pop smoke," Raymond said.

"Not yet."

"This is a hot zone, dude. We can't stay."

"What this is," Mick said, "is a crime scene. And we're the perps."

"What's the plan?"

"Your prisoner said the sergeant talked on the phone to people."

"Yeah."

"I want that phone."

Within ten minutes they'd inspected each body, none of which carried any identification. The oldest had gray hair and a slight belly. Mick figured he was the sergeant. Lying on the ground beside him was a Colt .45 pistol. His pocket held two cell phones.

"Need a piece of his shirt," Mick said.

Raymond withdrew a boot knife and cut off a section of fabric. Mick used it to pick up the pistol. He tucked it in the cargo pocket of his pants and examined the cell phones. One seemed to be for general use. The other had a history of calls from a single number. Mick called it. After three rings, a man answered with a terse voice.

"Russo?"

"No," Mick said. "Russo's dead. Everybody is dead."

"Who the fuck is this?"

"This is a warning call. You need to send a cleanup crew before the police get here."

"Put Russo on the line."

"Listen to what I'm saying. Russo's dead. The rest of the men are, too. How do you think I got this phone? It's a clusterfuck here. Total fubar. We need a chopper for the bodies."

The man on the other end was silent. Mick could hear his breathing.

"Sir," Mick said. "There's a cave filled with illegal toxic waste. That'll bring the Feds. It all leads right to Blacksword."

Mick ended the call.

"I need more cloth," he said to Raymond. "Make sure there's blood on it."

Mick pulled the dosimeter ring off the man's finger. Raymond sliced off sections of the dead man's shirt and handed them to Mick, who wiped the phone. Holding a corner of the phone he'd used, he wrapped the dead man's hand and fingers around it. He folded the bloody piece around the phone and stowed it in his pocket.

The other phone began to ring. Mick answered it.

"Same guy," Mick said. "Are the birds in the air? You don't get another warning. I'm *di di mau*."

He ended the call and tucked the phone away. Raymond was grinning.

"*Di di mau*?" he said. "Dude."

"I know. Figured old-school slang might throw them off."

"Can we bust a move now?"

Mick nodded, and they headed for the truck. He tossed the shovel and gloves in the bed, then strapped the suitcase against the low wall. He drove off the hill to the blacktop, went a few miles, and turned onto a narrow lane beneath heavy trees that made a canopy overhead. Raymond swept his vision from side to side, weapon poised, still in mission mode. A few miles later the road ended at the edge of Sand Plank Pay Lake. They threw their weapons and ammo into the water along with the shovel. After filling the gloves with rocks, they tossed them in, too.

Mick headed back across the county to the Kissick property. Neither spoke. Mick parked in the road to prevent disturbing Shifty's sleep.

"You think this'll come back on us?" Raymond said.

"My bet is Blacksword will clear the area. They have more to lose than we do."

"I don't like leaving all that toxic shit up there."

"I got a plan for that."

They looked at each other silently. Mick could tell that Raymond was considering whether to ask. Raymond shook his head to himself.

"Okay," he said. "Long as I'm out of it."

"I need a favor," Mick said. "A shower and clean clothes."

"You can't go home for that?"

"Prefer not. I stay with my sister right now. Shit, the election."

Mick turned on his phone and checked his texts—
three from Linda and one from Johnny Boy—Linda had
won the election. She'd be sheriff for the next four years.
Raymond got out of the truck.

"Come on," he said. "Don't use up all the hot water."

On the porch Mick undressed. Raymond showed him
the bathroom and Mick showered quickly. His torso was
scraped and bug-bit from crawling up the hill. He washed
his hair and toweled himself dry. A pile of mismatched
clothes lay on the floor. He found a set that mostly fit and
joined Raymond in the dim living room.

"Mason's shirt," Raymond said, "and Barney's pants.
I couldn't find a belt. I'll get rid of your clothes and boots.
Hang on, I forgot shoes."

Raymond went down the hall and returned with pairs
of cowboy boots, dress shoes, and Converse ball shoes.
Mick loosened the laces of the ball shoes and slipped them
on, knowing they'd stretch.

"You all right?" he said.

"No," Raymond said. "You?"

"I've seen worse. Done worse."

"Me, too. But these were US citizens."

"So were your brothers."

They looked at each other silently. There was nothing else for either of them to say. This would bind them
together forever, and they both wanted to get away. Mick
patted his damp hair in place around his ears.

"Very presentable," Raymond said. "You got a date?"

"No, of course not."

"You lying, dude? Yeah, you're lying. Is it Sandra? Tell her Ray-Ray said hey."

"I'm not saying anything about you. Best thing you and me can do is never see each other again."

"Got that right."

Raymond stuck his hand out.

"Not bad for army," Raymond said.

Mick nodded, shook his hand, and left. He moved the suitcase to the truck cab, then drove to town. The streets were empty, the stoplights flashing red, and he saw how easy it had been to dispose of Barney's body in the silent town. He parked in front of Sandra's house. The porch light glowed a soft yellow. From the front-room windows came the flickering of a television set. Mick gripped the door handle and hesitated, wondering if what he was doing made any sense at all. He'd stayed loyal to Peggy during their entire marriage. Now he wondered if he was fit for duty. One woman in eighteen years. Maybe that was it for him.

He strode across the yard with as much confidence as he could muster and gently tapped on the door, hoping Sandra wouldn't answer. After twenty seconds she opened the door.

"Heard your truck," she said. "Come on in."

He nodded and crossed the threshold.

Chapter Twenty-Four

Usually Mick awoke quickly, but today his return to the world was gradual. He was uncertain of his location other than an extremely comfortable bed. He felt more relaxed than he'd been in months. On the bedside table was a note from Sandra—she was running errands, Mick could eat anything in the kitchen, and she hoped to see him again. He rose, dressed, and left.

At his sister's house he changed into his own clothes. In a backyard firepit he burned the shirt and pants he'd borrowed from Raymond. He called the FBI field office in Louisville and asked for Special Agent Wilson. The switchboard put him on hold for fifteen minutes. He'd met Wilson the year before, when the agent had been assigned to assist with Linda's first homicide. In the way of privileged rookies, he'd managed to alienate Linda, Johnny Boy, and Mick. Locking up the wrong man had made things worse.

Wilson came on the line, his officious voice tinged by his standard resentment and a new world-weariness. Mick wondered if it was a pose, something learned from the old hands at the bureau.

"Special Agent Wilson here," he said.

"You looking to get back to DC?"

"Who is this?"

"The guy who's going to make your career."

"Identify yourself."

"Mick Hardin. Don't hang up."

"I owe you a sucker punch."

Mick swiftly told him about the toxic waste, the trucks from out of state, and Blacksword. He gave Wilson directions to the Mushroom Mines, emphasizing the need for hazmat suits and radiation detectors. He omitted the firefight.

"Is this on the level?" Wilson said. "I can't waste bureau resources on a wild-goose chase."

"When you get here, liaise with my sister. She'll have more details and potential evidence."

"Such as?"

"Cell phones, a weapon, DNA, and a dosimeter ring from the site. A couple of names."

"If you're fucking with me, I'll have you up on charges."

"I got to go. Got a flight back to base."

"Good riddance."

The phone clicked dead in Mick's ear. He went inside and made more coffee. He was pouring a cup when his sister came into the house.

"Congratulations, Sheriff," Mick said.

"Yeah, thanks. It's already a mess. I'm shorthanded, and Johnny Boy's on a call to Sharkey. Man says there's a wild hog out there killing cattle."

"I don't believe hogs do that."

"I don't either, but something damn sure killed them. He texted three pictures. I had to twist Johnny Boy's arm to go. He's worried we're getting cattle mutilations from UFOs."

"Coyotes," Mick said. "Or a pack of feral dogs."

"I know it. But he's got spaceships on the brain."

"Was he always like that?"

"He saw one when he was a kid. Then another a few years back."

"You believe him?"

"Mostly, I guess. He doesn't drink or do drugs. Other than being afraid of ghosts, he's pretty stable."

Mick nodded. A hummingbird inspected a morning glory vine with no blossoms, then moved on.

"You been up to something, Mick. Gone a lot and staying somewhere last night."

"First of all, last night's none of your business. Second, it was personal."

"Peggy?"

"No, she's still living with that guy."

"People get back together at the last minute sometimes."

"Not us," Mick said. "We're done."

"It's somebody though, isn't it?"

"Classified, Sis. Need to know."

"I'm glad you got your ashes hauled. I could use it myself."

"Uh . . ."

Linda grinned, enjoying his discomfort. Her cell phone chimed, and she answered. Mick made sandwiches while she listened on the phone and took notes. Linda ended the call, and they ate at their mother's old table, faded Formica with a metal band around the edges.

"That was Animal Control," she said. "They ruled out UFOs."

"What a relief."

"How's your leg?" she said.

"Healed up. Getting stronger."

"You never said what happened."

"Me and a buddy were trying to find a guy. He killed his girlfriend and went AWOL. We checked a village, but he wasn't there. On the way back to the Jeep, we got blowed up. My buddy died. Worst of it was, I saw who did it. A kid. Maybe ten or eleven years old. He was holding a phone and looking at me. He smiled right at me. Then *boom*."

She reached for his hand and squeezed it briefly.

"Sorry, Big Bro."

Mick nodded. He couldn't recall the last time his sister had touched him. Maybe a hug when their mother died. She withdrew her hand.

"Heard from the arson investigator with ATF," she said. "They'll be here this week."

Mick nodded. He went to his room for the cell phones, the .45 revolver, and the dosimeter ring. He set them on the table.

"This is from the guys who set the fire. Marquis dug a bullet out of Fuckin' Barney. The city police have it. My guess, it'll match this gun."

"Where'd you get all this?"

"It belonged to Russo, first name unknown, ex-military, rank of sergeant. You can ID him by fingerprints on the phone. If the records are expunged, the blood on the fabric has his DNA."

"Expunged?" she said.

"It's possible he's a black ops cipher. No official records."

"You need to tell me what's going on."

"It's about those Kissick boys and toxic waste. I don't know all the details."

"Bullshit, you don't. What toxic waste? Where?"

"The cell phones are Russo's, too. There's calls to Blacksword Security on one. The other has calls to Buckner Disposal, and a Mr. Knox."

"Knox?" she said. "As in Murvil?"

"It's possible he planted that heroin on Fuckin' Barney."

"This doesn't get any better."

"It gets worse," he said. "That FBI guy Wilson is coming."

"Why?"

"I called him."

Linda stood and walked in a tight circle. Mick recognized her fuming behavior and braced himself for the outcome. He was glad her hands were empty. She'd once thrown a ball-peen hammer through a car window.

"What the fucking fuck?" she said.

"There's my sister."

"I'm not your sister, I'm the sheriff."

"And I'm trying to help you," he said.

"By getting that Fed prick down here?"

"You'll get a lot of credit with the FBI and ATF. All the proof is right here on the table."

"When are you leaving?"

"Soon."

"Not soon enough."

She gathered the evidence and left the house. Mick washed the dishes, tidied his room, and put the sheets in the washing machine. On a shelf above it was a box of large garbage bags intended for yard debris. He put the blue suitcase in it. An Enterprise car rental was a few blocks away. The Converse shoes were surprisingly comfortable as he walked down Lyons Avenue, pulling a roller bag and carrying a garbage bag. He waved to Mr. Boyle, who was surveilling the street from his tiny porch.

Thirty minutes later Mick was heading for the interstate in a gray SUV. At Lexington he got on I-75 for the five-hour drive to Detroit. Inside the city limits he found a cheap hotel and checked into a room decorated in blue and silver. He booked a flight to Frankfurt-Hahn Airport for the following night. Abruptly exhausted, he undressed and slept for twelve hours.

The free breakfast buffet had been hit hard by a crew of construction workers, who'd consumed everything but the fruit. Mick ate a banana and drank two cups of coffee that surprised him with its strength. Returning to the room, he put the suitcase in the tub and rinsed off the clay mud. He toweled it dry, then used the complimentary blow-dryer on the hasps and hinges. It opened easily. Inside were four bricks of heroin wrapped in clear plastic and taped at the seams.

He called the Detroit number he'd gotten from Shifty's phone. It went to voice mail, which he expected, his own number being unknown to the recipient.

"I represent Barney Kissick in Kentucky," he said. "Tell Charley Flowers I need to speak to him."

He ended the call and looked out the window, wondering how long he'd have to wait. The parking lot was empty, except for his car and a work truck with a sign on

256 CHRIS OFFUTT

the door for Bea Day Plumbing. On a small table lay a few brochures for tourist sites—music, barbeque, and art galleries. Another booklet featured the Henry Ford Museum, the holdings of which included Thomas Edison's last breath in a sealed tube and an Oscar Mayer Wienermobile.

Fifteen minutes later the phone rang, and Mick answered immediately.

"Who's this?" the caller said.

"I got this number from Mrs. Kissick. I'm her friend."

"What do you want?"

"Charley Flowers."

"He ain't here."

"In that case give him a message."

Mick waited. After thirty seconds the other man spoke.

"What's the message?"

"Tell Mr. Flowers if he ain't there, then neither is his property."

Mick hung up before the guy could speak. Two minutes later the phone rang again. Mick answered.

"Mr. Flowers?" he said.

"No. I'm—"

Mick ended the call before the man could finish. He wondered how long this pattern would continue. Mick could do it for the next seven hours until his flight. Outside, a woman was removing a heavy-duty basin wrench from the plumbing truck. The phone rang.

"Mr. Flowers?" Mick said.

"Yes," said a man's hard voice.

"I have something of yours. Something you gave Barney Kissick. He's dead. I'm willing to return your property. An exchange."

He waited again, longer this time. Charley Flowers had more discipline than his minions. Still, Mick knew he'd want further information.

"Exchange for what?" Flowers said.

"Leave Mrs. Kissick alone."

"That's all you want?"

"Yes, sir, it is."

"What's your angle?"

"None," Mick said. "I'm a friend of the family."

"If I agree. And I repeat, *if*. When do I get the property?"

"I'm in Detroit now."

"Nine o'clock tonight."

"I'll be gone then. My timetable is strict."

"What are you, a politician?"

"No, sir. I have a flight."

"Back to Kentucky?"

"I suggest we meet in the cell phone lot at DTW. Plenty of people around."

"There's two. North and South."

"Your choice, Mr. Flowers."

"North. Three o'clock."

"All right."

"How will my man know you?" Flowers said.

"Text this number when he's in the lot. I'll flash my lights."

"If this is a trick, you die."

"No trick, Mr. Flowers. I don't want Mrs. Kissick to suffer."

Flowers ended the call, and Mick put his phone away. He went to the lobby and asked for the nearest restaurant and was enthusiastically informed about a chicken and waffle place next door. After eating, he returned to his room and rested for a couple of hours. He transferred the bricks of heroin into the garbage bag, then loaded his car. He drove below the speed limit, veering around potholes, some containing pieces of plastic broken from cars. He passed empty lots filled with weeds, strip malls of hipster shops, then a neighborhood of abandoned buildings beside high-end condos. At a renovation site he threw the empty blue suitcase in a dumpster.

He took Middlebelt to Goddard, then turned on Service Road, arriving an hour early. The lot was smaller than he'd expected, laid out in a circular fashion, with one way in and out. Every vehicle was American, most made by Detroit car companies. He found a spot near the exit and parked, nose out. There were two open spaces beside him, then a midsize sedan. Nobody sat behind the wheel, unusual for a cell phone lot. Mick wondered if it was a setup. He put the car in gear, prepared to abort the mission. A partially nude man climbed from the back seat to the front. A few seconds later, a woman got out the back door and into the passenger side. She peered into the visor mirror while applying lipstick. The man was grinning as they drove away.

Mick watched the entrance, holding the Beretta. The garbage bag was on the passenger seat. A minivan entered, and three cars left. At five minutes before three, a late-model Cadillac drove slowly in, circled the lot as Mick had done, and backed into a spot opposite him. The driver wore a Lions hat sideways on his head. The passenger pressed numbers into a cell phone. He finished and looked up. Mick recognized him as Vernon Armstrong. Charley Flowers had sent him and another man into the hills the year before to scare Mick, an undertaking that had backfired. Mick was surprised that Vernon was still around, although of the pair, he had been the smarter.

Mick's phone buzzed with a text that read: *We here where you at*.

Mick responded: *Right in front of you*.

Vernon read it and looked through the windshield.

Mick flashed his lights, then typed: *I got the stuff. Come get it*.

The Cadillac door opened. Vernon walked warily across the blacktop and stopped halfway. Mick lowered his window and poked his head out.

"Hey, Vernon, remember me?"

"Oh, fuck," Vernon said. "Not you again."

"How's your buddy? Freddie, right?"

"He's dead."

"I didn't figure he'd last long in your business."

"It wasn't like that. He had a stroke."

"Young as he was?"

"Yeah, nobody believes it. But I was there. He went down like a stuck hog. We were in line at a Coney. I had to call nine-one-one, then split."

"I guess Charley moved you up."

"I'm handling more, yeah. You really giving that dope back?"

Mick nodded. He leaned across the cab, opened the passenger door, and shoved the garbage bag onto the pavement. The Cadillac driver propped a pistol on the side mirror, aimed at Mick. Vernon took a step toward the bag.

"Not yet," Mick said. "Tell your buddy to put his pistol away."

Vernon turned and motioned with his hand. The driver pulled his hand back into the car.

"Can he shoot that way?" Mick said.

"Yeah. He's left-handed. Shocks the shit out of people when he rolls up shooting. Best shot I ever seen."

"I'll take your word for it. I'm going to drive out of here now. Don't worry, the dope's in the bag. Tell your buddy not to try anything stupid."

"You can't tell him nothing."

"I can. But he won't like the way I tell him. Charley won't either."

Vernon thought a few seconds, then walked to the driver's side of the Cadillac and spoke. He returned to the

garbage bag, checked its contents, looked at Mick, and gestured toward the exit. Mick eased forward, turning the
wheel to leave, then stopped.

"One more thing," he said.

"What now?"

"The roads up here. Why're they so bad?"

"Long winter and a lot of cars."

Mick nodded.

"See you later, Vernon."

"I fucking hope not."

The Enterprise rental return office was a half mile
away. Mick drove past it to Hertz and waited, in case Vernon followed him. Satisfied that he hadn't, Mick drove to
Enterprise and parked. At the counter he turned in the keys
and took the shuttle to Concourse A. He wiped the Beretta
down, dropped it in a trash can, and put the clip in another
one. From there he caught a tram that carried him to the
international terminal. If someone found the pistol, they'd
start out looking in the wrong place.

He texted Raymond: *Done. Your mom is safe.*

A minute later Raymond texted back: *Thanks.*

Mick erased the text history, a precaution if he was
detained. Being careful meant thinking like a criminal, a
skill at which he excelled. It had helped his career, but at
times he wondered if he was drifting too far in that direction. Mick had paid four thousand dollars for a last-minute
first-class ticket and joined a line to pass through the intri-
cacies of international security. His military identification

would have hastened the procedure, but many TSA workers were veterans, and most veterans didn't like CID. Active soldiers didn't either. Nobody really did, and now neither did he. He'd become what he despised, a retribution killer.

On the plane he stared through the oval window and tried to refocus his thoughts. He'd stopped the dumping of toxic waste. He'd rehabbed his leg, placed campaign signs for his sister, and found out who killed the Kissick brothers. He'd made Peggy happy with divorce. He'd gotten Charley Flowers off Shifty's back and helped Jaybird out of his Dollar General mess. The list was too short for all the bloodshed left behind. Twelve people dead, and here he was bragging to himself about little things. He wondered how often people tried to convince themselves that homicide was acceptable in service to the greater good. He knew better. The greater good didn't exist except as an excuse.

Mick buckled himself in and feigned sleep until the plane was in the air. Tension drained from his limbs. He invariably felt better when leaving one place and heading to another. He fit in best in foreign countries, where being an outsider was perfectly normal. Aside from that he was comfortable on an airplane or alone in the woods.

Acknowledgments

The author is grateful to the following people for assistance during the writing of this book: Kathi Whitley, Jonathan Lethem, Randy Ryan, and Melissa Ginsburg.